Indivisible Hearts

by Cece Whittaker

Easton One Productions
Absecon, New Jersey
www.CeceWhittakerStories.com
First Edition, 2019.

Cover Photography © by Thomas Klee, 2019
Instagram: @tom.klee; https://500px.com/tomklee

Cover Design by Easton One Productions
https://ccword.wixsite.com/editandco/our-services

ISBN 13: 9781697702279

Chapter One

Bernice's short feathery hair lifted up and down in the offshore bluster, despite her efforts to catch it up in her red woolen scarf, as she scurried down 23rd Street. There was no cure for the wild, ever-present, South Jersey wind. But on that fall afternoon in 1944, the wind was the least of her worries.

There was the war, for one thing. Abbottsville itself was showing a little war-wear. But it was not from shelling and broken buildings. It was more from the steady surge of hearts broken by bad, even terminal news. Bernice worried that the blue uniformed Western Union bicyclist might appear with one of those terrible telegrams in hand.

Around the corner from Bernice, at 6 North Edison Street, 21-year-old Joan bustled into the embracing warmth of Helen Ashenbach's house.

"Anybody home?" she called weakly.

The waver in her voice brought Helen out of the kitchen in a hurry. "Joan? Everything all right?"

"I got a letter," Joan said, dropping her coat on the rug and embracing Helen. "He's not coming back home. He's shipping to Okla--" her voice dropped into a gulp. "homa."

The heartbreaking stories of wartime romances were no stranger to Helen. Her husband, Harry, had marched through World War I but nevertheless had felt compelled to enter the fray a second time in the current punishing violence.

"Oh honey, I'm so sorry," Helen said, wrapping Joan up in her arms. "But things usually have a way of working out, and of course it could be worse." She knew her platitudes were weak, but they nearly always seemed to be true. And poor Joan. She took things so hard.

Just as Bernice reached Helen's house, Annie shot ahead of her on the steps of the front porch. "Well look at that energy!" Annie said. "What kind of lunches are they serving at the convents these days?"

"Very funny," said Bernice. "But I wasn't at the convent. I was just merrily enjoying this wonderful weather." She knocked on Helen's door, then went in without waiting to be asked.

"*Wonderful?*" said Annie, left behind on the steps.

"Oh, look at this! Two for the price of one," called Helen. "So we're all here. Come in. Have you two heard Joan's news?"

Annie nodded as she took off her coat, releasing her long, dark tresses. She was tall and slim, an Italian-American beauty. "It's torture," she said, the length of the first syllable more than double the length of the second. "It aint fair."

Bernice joined Helen and Joan in their hug. But then when she noticed Joan's tears, she backed away and began dancing an absurd little jig, batting her eyelashes. "You still have us!" she said to Joan.

Joan smiled reluctantly, then burst into laughter, then cried, then laughed again. "It's not like it's anything new," she said mournfully, "and at least I am getting a letter from *him*, and not the Army."

The others nodded. That was true enough. Too many of the neighbors and parishioners had lost loved ones since the men had begun to march off. Silver and gold stars adorned the homes of those willing to tell that story, while others, too grief stricken, just closed within, not sharing their pain with anyone, as if it were the last of what existed between them and their men.

"I've got something that will cheer you up," Annie offered, showing them a parcel. "Ma sent this over to add her thanks for the clean-up."

Annie's family owned the DiRosa Bakery in neighboring Atlantic City. Despite the war, the bakery was growing in popularity, due largely to the increasing population of wounded and their families temporarily residing at the Veteran's Hospital. The local government had determined that even though sugar was scarce and needed to be rationed, businesses would be less subject to the rationing. It was good news to Annie's family, and ultimately, Annie's friends.

"Oh, we didn't do anything," said Bernice, reaching shamelessly for the box.

"Maybe *you* didn't, but me and Joanie did, and Helen, too," said Annie. "Get your hands off. I'll open it."

"I'm just helping," Bernice said. One thing she could not seem to defeat was an overwhelming weakness for sweets. That fondness was reflected in her moderately round figure, accentuated by her equally moderately lower stature.

"It looks like something good and fattening," said Helen, her 58 years sounding very motherly, "but not before dinner."

"Awww," said Annie.

Joan laughed. "Well, at least let us see what it is. We can't gain any weight by looking."

Annie undid the tape around the edges and opened the pastry box to reveal a beautiful, thick-layered cheesecake, topped with multi-colored icing forming the American flag.

"Ooooh!" said Joan.

"I don't know if I can wait. . ." Bernice said.

"If Helen says we gotta, we gotta," said Annie.

"Oh my," said Helen. "Close that up before I get out a knife and fork!"

The autumn of 1944 had seen one of South Jersey's worst hurricanes on record. While there were blessedly fewer trees at the shore community than one would see inland, there was still plenty of mess. Flattened shrubberies, broken glass, trash cans overturned, and even seaweed spread clear across the island. There had also been severe injury and even lives lost.

Atlantic City's large convention hall had been converted into the veterans hospital. Its presence could not have been more opportune in the aftermath of the hurricane. While Annie's family had been spared, many of the locals had been injured, unaware of the impending rancor of the storm.

Volunteering at the hospital, Helen had shared her unshakable good humor, doing little chores like delivering supplies to the nursing nuns, and sorting patient records and files. With the worst of the emergency behind them, her service was coming to an end.

"Helen, I hope I can cook as well as you one day," Joan said, lingering as she cleared the table. The roast chicken dinner that night, a rare and wonderful thing those days, had been slowly but enthusiastically consumed.

"I hear you do a pretty amazing casserole already," Helen said.

"She does!" Annie agreed, collecting the utensils. She and Joan shared a rented house only blocks from Helen's. "I can vouch for you, Joanie! Dick will not stay lean for long after you two get married."

Joan smiled. What a marvelous thought; creating menus, collecting good recipes, and returning her man to a healthy weight. She wondered how he was feeling that night and when he would be returned to the United States. She thought about the delicious chicken she had just enjoyed, wishing she could have shared it with Dick.

"Hello? Lost in thoughts?" Annie said, taking the plates from her.

"Yes," Joan answered dreamily. Poor Annie, she thought suddenly. Her Sylvester was so far away, and in his letters, there was no indication that he would be home any time soon. Joan, Annie, Bernice, and Helen had struggled all summer with thoughts about the war impossible to fend off. The men had been incommunicado since late that summer. It was only

recently that Joan learned that Dick was going to be all
right. She knew very little of the details, but it was clear
that he had suffered some sort of injury. He had been
"out of action," as he described it in his letters, for
quite some time.

Joan wondered how it was that Dick had already
received orders. "I guess they take turns" is all Helen
had said. Joan knew that with Helen's experience, she
probably had some inkling of the fuller story, and that
story's mystery kept Joan on edge. But fear
discouraged her from asking questions.

In the kitchen, Joan ran the warm water into the
ceramic sink and shook a few dish detergent flakes into
it. The others didn't like doing the dishes, but she
loved it. The warm, sudsy water making the dishes
bright and clean again gave her a special kind of joy.
Helen had set the rack up beside the sink, with the little
drain board underneath, slanting so that the water
from the dishes would drain back into the sink.

Helen's dishes were so pretty. They had used the
blue and white ones that night, so Joan was extra
careful not to let any of them slip out of her hands.

Another part of the pleasure of washing dishes was
seeing the beautiful paintings on them show through
again. In that instance, the paintings were of children
and their parents under a wide, leafy tree, in the midst
of a field, enjoying a picnic. Joan liked to imagine what
was in the basket. Was it fried chicken? Or rich meat
and cheese sandwiches on fluffy white bread? Or bread
with apple butter and bottles of fresh, cold milk?

"You take such good care of my dishes," Helen
said, wiping down the counter tops. "You'll do just fine
when you are married." She gave Joan a little hug and

took the dishrag into the dining room to wipe down the table.

I hope so, thought Joan. She could just see their wedding. She would wear a beautiful ivory and lace gown, studded with pearls and thick taffeta petticoats. The sleeves would be long and dainty, and the edged lace would reach all the way down to her knuckles. She imagined her beautiful groom. Tall and sleek, thick dark-haired, smiling Dick Thimble in a black and white tuxedo. It was heaven to imagine.

As Joan's fancy found her a moment of happiness, Dick Thimble's stretcher was carefully extracted from the belly of a Douglas C-47 Skytrain at Ft. Sill, Oklahoma.

"He looks like he survived the trip, anyway," a medic said as he prepared to receive the cargo.

"Well, keep a close eye," said the attending physician. "The infection that set in back at the post was pretty universal. He seems to have rallied but get him set up as soon as possible. I'll have a word with your on-duty. Gotta get that fever down."

Several other patients were wheeled down the ramp, through the passageway into the transport vehicles as well before the giant cargo plane slowly rumbled into position to be refueled. In less than an hour, another heroic crew would lift off to deliver supplies and equipment, and, in God's mercy, return home again bearing more injured American warriors.

Dick Thimble's once merry and mischievous eyes were closed and motionless. His bones were barely covered, the only noticeable flesh being on his tenacious muscular shoulders. His pallor and stillness were punctuated only by an occasional shuddering. The green sheets covering him were ominously reflective of those used to recover and store the bodies of comrades in arms lost.

But Dick's lungs still moved, his heart still pumped. There was motion; there was life. There was hope.

Chapter Two

They'll think I don't have anything to do at home, Helen thought smiling to herself as she got off the elevator. The hospital was in full swing, but somehow it still felt like the convention center.

"It's certainly got enough lights for a hospital," Helen said softly to herself, admiring the brightness. She welcomed the warm and well-lit corridors after the wind and chill outside. The bus stop was several long blocks away from the hospital. She didn't relish making the return journey an hour later.

The days were growing shorter and seemed to be overcast most of the time. If it wasn't raining, it was due to, or even dropping ice pellets that made travel impossible. But a deal was a deal, and she had promised to finish out her volunteer time.

Her supervisor had set up a table for them and was busily sorting through the files that still needed to be arranged in alphabetical order. Their contents, too, needed to be arranged, but in chronological order.

"Good morning, Helen!" she called. "We're all set up in here. Would you like a cup of coffee? I know it's brisk out there."

"That sounds heavenly!" said Helen.

As the two sat companionably sorting and organizing the files, her supervisor shook her head. "So many things gone wrong with these boys," she said. "They're just kids, you know, Helen."

"Oh yes, that's what makes it so tragic."

"This one here, he's been here a week already and he's doing fine. A rough break on the battlefield, but he's coming along all right. But he won't let anyone know he's here. It's up to them to allow notification to their families, and he just won't do it."

Helen shook her head. "Battle fatigue?"

"Well, there might be more to it than that," her supervisor said. "He's got a nasty leg injury. His doctor says it could go either way."

"Oh, he might lose it?"

"He might. But he might also keep it. Here, you look through, and organize that one. I'm going down to the nurses' desk for a minute."

Helen took the file. The poor fellow, she thought. She shook the contents of the file onto the tabletop in front of her. On the admission form she read Robert R. McGarrett, age 24, place of birth, Washington, D.C. That's funny, she thought, being from Washington, he could be one of the young men who came to the dances at St. Nick's last year. His record was lengthy and involved. He'd been overseas, wounded in France, then treated in England before being brought to the US. It looked like, yes, ten days.

As Helen turned the page to the next form, she suddenly froze. My stars! she thought, Robert McGarrett, that's Laureen's young man, that's Bob! It has to be. There can't be two—not both from Washington, D.C.!

Her supervisor was returning to the table, two cups of coffee resting on top of yet more stacks of files. "How are you coming along?" she asked Helen.

"Listen," Helen said, tapping the file folder, "this soldier. Would it be all right if I visited him?"

"Sure, Helen, but as I said, he's having a pretty rough time of it. I'll take you back there."

As they traveled the hall toward Bob's room, one of the nuns attending patients on Bob's ward stopped them and asked who they wanted.

"I'll leave you in the good hands of Sister Dorothy Marie," Helen's supervisor said. "Come back and let me know how it went, will you?"

"I surely will," said Helen.

She tried to come up with a casual greeting for Bob as she followed Sister to his room. Her impulsive decision to visit a man she hardly knew at a very low point in his life was catching up with her. Maybe it's uncomfortable, she thought, but it's the right thing to do.

That particular hall was more softly lit, and much quieter than the bright bustling downstairs. Muted groans and rapidly moving rubber soles on the marble floor did little to ease Helen's mild panic. Sister's habit swooshed as she moved ahead of Helen, occasionally looking into some of the rooms.

At the end of the hall, she stopped and entered a room, indicating the bed in which Bob lay. A green drape hung suspended in a U-shape around his bed, which Sister gently pulled to one side. It created a partial opening, to which she brought forward a chair.

"Please stay as long as you like," she said. "If he only sleeps and you can't converse, he, as well as all of these men, can always use your prayers."

"Yes, of course," said Helen. "Thank you very much."

She set down her pocketbook, scooting the chair a little closer before sitting down. She had seen only Bob's back, as he lay facing the opposite wall. But she could clearly see that one leg was braced and thickly bandaged just above the knee and all the way down to the ankle.

Helen drew in her breath. While she was no stranger to war injuries, this young man's plight immediately tore at her heart. At almost the same instant that she spotted his injury, Helen could remember the smiling, self-assured, very handsome young man so clearly in love with his girlfriend, Laureen. As her tears gathered and dropped onto the sheets below, she was grateful that he had been sleeping.

She wiped her eyes and nose, and silently prayed for mercy. *Remember oh most Gracious Virgin Mary, that never was it known, that anyone who fled to thy protection, implored thy help, or sought thy intercession was left unaided.* It was then that she saw a modest rustling under the sheets.

Slowly Bob rolled onto his back. He seemed to know that someone was there, but he did not look in her direction. Instead, he said in a very monotone voice, "Nothing, thanks. I'll wait for dinner."

Helen remained in place, partly to give him a chance to look at her, and recognize her, and partly at a loss for what else to do.

But Bob remained motionless. After a few moments, he said, "I don't mean to be rude, but I'd like to be alone."

Something about the slight animation in his voice gave Helen the opening that she needed.

"Bob," she said warmly.

Bob turned to face her. Her face didn't register at first. He squinted and seemed to be trying to focus for a moment. Then he leaned forward, seemingly heartened and curious at the same time. "Oh, Mrs. Ashenbach," he said, with the slightest hint of a smile. "Long time."

Helen nodded. "Yes. So very long. It is good to see you again."

St. Benedict's Roman Catholic Church stood on a busy corner in Abbottsville, where newspaper boys alongside shoeshines and one florist had set up shop. The church's ornately stained-glass windows sparkled on a sunny day, drawing at least passing admiration from pedestrians.

To Annie, though, they were a wealth of inspiration. Inside St Benedict's, the gentle flicker of the candles brought out the deeper beauty of the artwork. The detail in the scenes of Christ's Passion and Resurrection had been ornately crafted years before in a small village in Italy. The rich silver blue color of the sky always caught Annie's eye.

The church was dimly lit inside. The soft scent of the wax and lingering incense seemed to embrace her heart in a gentle welcome. Annie slowly approached and genuflected, her large purse and knitting bag clunking gracelessly against her as she did so. As she drew closer to the rack of candles, several of which were already lit for special intentions, she felt stronger than she had in weeks, months even. The climate inside her heart was warming, growing more secure.

One candle sat far from those lit, seeming to beckon from within its tall, royal blue translucent glass, and Annie complied. She struck a long match, lit the candle, dropped a coin into the box, and knelt before the statue of the Madonna and Child.

Her silent prayers offered thanks for her blessings as well as for the many times she'd succeeded in avoiding the darkness of despair over the preceding months. She thought of Joan, Helen, and Bernice, and prayed for them as well. Her final prayer was for the possessor of her heart, Sylvester Bapini, whose exact whereabouts were unknown. *Bless him and Keep him safe.*

Then, as if clicking a switch, Annie stood up quickly, gathered her belongings and hurried to the back of the church which connected her to the path through to the Vesper Shop. *Her* vesper shop, to be exact. Annie had been handed the keys by her uncle before he enlisted, with the assurance that it would remain hers for as long as she wanted it.

Her Uncle Paulie had seen an opportunity years before, and being a gifted businessman, he'd taken it. But Paulie's affinity for sacred statues, prayers, and vespers in general was not well developed. So Annie worked diligently to slowly reduce the clutter of old calendars and unidentifiable statues. She created instead a specialty shop of Catholic objet d'art, including statuary, paintings, less expensive reprints in "holy card" form, prayer missiles, and gifts suitable for the many Sacramental celebrations. Joan had accused her of curating only along the lines of Italian art. Annie argued, but it was true. Annie loved her heritage, despite the few nobblers that had snuck in. What was a family without a few bad apples anyway, she thought.

As she lifted the sheets from the glass cases, and then dusted the statues beyond her reach with the long-handled feather duster, she toyed with the idea of setting up a display on top of the one glass case to the side. Just for Christmas time, though, she decided. But she knew she would have to start ordering right then or nothing would arrive on time.

Christmas, she thought. She leaned back against the glass case and closed her eyes. When she really tried, she could still feel Sylvester's muscular arms around her. He'd been wounded the previous Christmas, and that wound had given him the great blessing of a stateside pass.

"I thought I told you not to get hit," she had said to him after they'd had some time together.

He had smiled. "Hey listen, I meant to steer clear, but I just had to find out what it was like."

Annie laughed, her rich brown eyes full of the glistening light of true love. "Well, watch it," she had said. "You do that again and you'll have to answer to me."

"Hey, nobody wants that to happen!" he had said laughing, his dark brown eyes shining.

As she rested against the display cases, Annie smiled, the conversation so fresh and heartening in her mind. Yet, it had been just that conversation that had sent her to the edge of despair later as she'd waited months to hear from him. *Nobody wants that to happen.*

"You got that right," she said out loud. "And it won't, as long as you remember what I told you, Bapini."

She wasn't fooling herself, yet somehow she felt better taking a pseudo-tough stance. It made her laugh and at the same time made her feel strong.

She looked through a catalog and decided on a few items to order. Annie spotted a modest but beautiful Nativity Scene, including some unusual characters, such as a sheepdog, and two young boys in Middle Eastern clothing. The artist had tried to conceive a little fuller picture of the visitors to the Christ Child. That type of thinking appealed to Annie, and the artwork was beautiful. She giggled out loud to discover his name—Francesco Nardini. *I'm going to hear about this from Joanie,* she thought.

"I can't help it if I like Italian art," she said out loud, as she wrote out the order.

"You are certainly entitled to have that opinion," a slightly monotone voice responded.

Annie looked up to see Margaret poking her head in the door. Margaret was another single girl who worked at the church part time. She wore her hair straight, chin length, and parted in the middle. She had a wardrobe and a way of walking that, combined with her physical appearance, never failed to remind Annie of Prince Valiant.

"Oh hello, Margaret," she said, in a charitable tone.

"Good morning, Ann," Margaret responded, adjusting her heavy dark-rimmed glasses. "There's no reason to apologize for your affection for Italian art."

"Oh, no, I know it. I was just imagining Joanie saw it and—"

"Joan isn't Italian of course," said Margaret, as if closing the subject.

"Well, no—"

"I was wondering if I could discuss a personal matter with you," Margaret bulldozed ahead.

Annie was startled. Margaret was not one to share personal feelings. In fact, amongst the other girls, there was a little doubt as to the existence of emotion beyond her exacting and almost robotic attempts at conversation. "Of course," she said.

"Very good," said Margaret. "This is the situation. Through much of the summer I have not had a boyfriend, probably thanks in part to your friend, Bernice."

"I don't think Bernice—" Annie said, but was quickly interrupted.

"No matter," said Margaret. "Whosever fault it was, I'm ready to engage again. So do you know anyone who's looking?"

Annie had to think for a minute. It was not unusual for a girl to ask to be set up with a fellow. But by that time, asking wasn't necessarily getting. In fact, there were very few eligible men left anywhere in the US except for on military bases. She thought of the soldiers at the hospital and those who marched on the beaches in Atlantic City. But somehow, they seemed a little worldly for Margaret, maybe a little over her head.

"I will have to think about that, Margaret," she finally said. "But I don't know of anyone off-hand."

"Fine," Margaret said nodding, as if closing a business deal. "At least I've put the bee in your bonnet."

Annie smiled, almost expecting her to reach for a handshake. "And I'll pass the word, okay Margaret?"

"Thank you."

After Margaret had marched back out, Annie tried to imagine the kind of man that would be suited to her. The boyfriend she'd alluded to from the previous year was a very lightweight character. Friendly enough, but not what Annie considered to have been a good match. The fact that he'd disappeared seemed to confirm that.

A few boxes had come in during the slow time for the shop, and Annie had set them in the back. As she pulled one of them from the stack, she thought she heard a noise. Maybe a shifting of some of the boxes, she thought. It had been some time since she'd been back there. I'd better be careful to make sure they don't all fall over, she thought.

Later, Annie locked up and exited the church, stepping into the wind tunnel Abbottsville residents had come to accept as autumn. Bundling up tighter inside her thick burgundy wool coat, she caught sight of Helen just stepping off the bus.

It was easy to spot her friend, who had switched recently from wearing a lined raincoat to her bright blue wool coat, with a deep hood.

"Helen!" she called out, her voice cutting through the wind. "Wait, I'll walk with you."

Helen turned around smiling, recognizing Annie's voice. "Great timing, I guess!" she said. "Is Joan with you?"

"No, I think she's home working on the crafts."

"Wise girl! I had planned to come home a lot sooner," Helen said as they crossed 23rd Street together. "But I got caught up in things at the hospital." She had not yet decided whether or not to tell the girls about Bob. She wondered if maybe her first duty was to Laureen, or Bob's family.

"It was your last day, huh?" said Annie. The wind had stirred up and was whipping at their words. Annie reached up to try to tie her scarf more securely around her neck.

"Here, let me help," said Helen. "Yes, I think it was supposed to be my last day, but they might want me to help out until I finish a project I was working on." She hoped her evasive answer would be enough.

"You're too good, Helen!" Annie said. "I bet they're walking around in circles wondering what they're going to do without ya!"

Helen laughed as they parted. "See you again soon!" she called, heading down North Edison Street.

It was only a little ways further to Annie and Joan's house, but the wind had grown so wild, Annie had to fight to stay upright. She hoped Helen was already safely inside her home. Annie thought of the soldiers suddenly, and felt grateful to be on land, and not at sea during that kind of weather. The thought of it made her shiver as she climbed the porch steps.

She grabbed at the knob as it flung open, but ended up chasing the door inside, trying to catch it before the wind slammed it against the inside wall. She caught her heel on a stubble of the carpet, lost her balance and collapsed like a bag of potatoes against the open door.

Bernice appeared with her hands on her hips. "Graceful," she said.

"Get me a cup of something hot," Annie said getting up. "What are you doin' here?"

"We're just gabbing!" Joan called from the kitchen. "Tea okay?"

"Sounds great."

Annie hung up her coat and scarf and settled onto the couch. "It's getting dark really early these days," she said. "I'm so glad your dad put up those lights." Joan's father owned the house they rented. He was like a second father to Annie and took great pains to maintain their little house.

"Here you go," said Joan. "Bernice was hoping you'd be bringing home some goodies."

"That the only reason you're here?" Annie asked.

Bernice decided not to answer. "All right," she said, "if you're going to be mean to me, I won't tell you my news."

"You inherited another million bucks," said Annie, sipping her tea. "But you want me and Joanie to have it."

Bernice shook her head. As funny as it sounded, Bernice was, in fact, a millionaire. She had never intended to be one, and certainly had not done anything to earn her riches. But over the summer, she had experienced a dramatic elevation in financial stature. When visiting her uncle's lawyer following his death, and expecting to be gifted with a chiming clock, she went home with the news that she'd become a wealthy woman.

Nobody knew that Uncle Louis had amassed a fortune. Not even his sister-in-law, Bernice's mother. With Bernice's steadfast aspiration toward the Sacred life as a nun, she viewed her new status as more of a project than a party.

For weeks, she had struggled with the chore of determining how to get rid of the money in a most judicious, prudential, and in keeping with Bernice's person, loving manner. Paying off her mother's mortgage had been an easy first step, followed by accommodating her beloved convent of Sisters into a larger, stronger, and better situated building. A trust that would support the Sisters' utility needs came next, along with the establishment of a food and expenses budget that would go directly to the Mother Superior.

Their local parish priest, Father Bertrand, and a visiting priest from Lithuania, Monsignor Kuchesky, had assisted in many ways with Bernice's efforts, which stepped slightly outside of the regular regimen of financial flow between the Dioceses. But once those feathers had been smoothed, Bernice had turned her attention to the local situation.

A middle-aged grocer with a heart of gold had followed that heart in the dispensing of groceries to local folks on a credit basis throughout the previous decade. Unfortunately, even with the turn of events into the war, grocery bills remained unpaid, and the grocer was facing bankruptcy. Just that afternoon, Bernice had offered to buy the store and its contents at a generous price.

"No," Bernice said, answering Annie's question, "I didn't get more money. But the Abbottsville Grocer is not going under."

Joan took a seat on the couch next to Annie, her eyes shining. She hated change, and the idea of the store going out of business had been plaguing her for weeks. "Tell us, tell us!" she said.

Bernice sat down. "I don't know how it will all work," she said, "but my idea is to sell to those who can pay, and sneak food packages to those who can't."

"You're going to have to do some fancy sneakin'," Annie said. "Nobody's going to want it known that they're not able to buy their own groceries."

"Worse yet, be seen as charity cases," Joan added.

"You're right," said Bernice. "That's what I mean, I don't know how it will work. We have to keep it secret, just between us and whoever delivers the stuff."

"And Helen," said Joan.

"Well, yes, of course Helen," said Bernice, "and Father. We won't even know where the food boxes should go without *their* help. I want everyone that we can possibly reach to be helped out, maybe once or twice a month. I don't know if it's logical or if a tiny grocery store can even do that, but I want to try."

"I love it!" said Joan. "Let's get Helen over!"

"We're going there for dinner again, remember?" said Annie.

"That's one thing," said Bernice. "This probably isn't going to go a long way to improve *our* food situation." She looked at Joan and Annie. "But we'll have enough."

Chapter Three

In a tent in a small town in Italy, three American soldiers sat listening to the rain and playing cards.

"I could use a sandwich," said a tall, dark-haired lieutenant leaning against a sack of semolina flour. "With pickles, lots of pickles and olives. Oregano, oil, that nice grated cheese. . ."

"Yeah Sly, you're missing the good stuff, the main ingredients. What good's a sangwich without the meat?" his buddy Bobby answered.

"Look, we're lucky to get *this* stuff, what's it called? Expresso? So just be grateful. Our guys are out there in the snow," said Captain Harry Ashenbach.

The other two men were startled by their CO's stern reprimand.

"Sorry, Cap," said Bobby, the shorter of the two. "Just talkin'."

"Yeah Harry," added Sly. "Didn't mean to ruffle no feathers."

Harry stood up in the small tent and stretched his legs to release the tension. "Forget it. I'm edgy. By the way, Bobby, how come you always say 'sangwich?'"

Bobby looked at Sly, then back at his boss. "What do you mean, why do I always say sangwich? I only said it 'cause Sly was talking about it. *He* brung it up."

"Yeah, he brought up the subject, but why do ya say 'sangwich?'"

Bobby shook his head and put out his hands. "I don't get it."

Sly chuckled. "Yeah, Bobby, how come you always talk about food?"

"*You* was the one 'at started it." Bobby was getting irritated.

"He don't know he says it that way," Sly said to Harry.

"Look, if you want, we can talk about the weather. But I like food as much as the next guy. And I'd rather talk about that."

"I wonder how them other guys is making out," said Sly. "You know, Dick, Joan's fella. I think their division was headed for France. Had to be involved in them beach landings."

"I haven't met him," said Bobby. "But I feel for them guys. That was ugly. But they did it, man. They're really knocking on old Adolf's door."

Harry sighed. "Yeah, that is a grim business. Still going on, I'm sure. But right now, I don't feel like talking about that."

"Yeah, me neither," said Bobby.

"I'd rather talk about Annie, or maybe I wouldn't," Sylvester said. "Not sure you guys should be in on that discussion."

Bobby chuckled. "Hey, whatever you wanna say. . . Course, this rainy season back again, I'm guessing the mail service is pretty much dead." He didn't want to ask Harry when they should expect the mail service to return. It made him feel like a kid at home, asking repeatedly how many days 'til my birthday? Or when is it going to snow? How could he ever have loved snow, he wondered. And would he ever love it again?

"You got that right," Harry said sighing. "Helen's probably given up on me by now." Harry had been relieved pending replacement, but he kept that news to himself. Besides, to date, no replacement had ever been located. At times, he worried that the Army was content to keep him where he was. He loved serving his country, but he missed his home; his church, his easy chair, and most of all, his wife.

"Oh yeah, that ain't happening." Sly knew the remarkable history of Harry and his wife Helen. She was a pillar of strength with a sense of humor and a genius in the kitchen. And she had more love for her fellow than he thought he'd ever seen before.

Harry smiled slightly, nodding.

"I'd like to know how Debbie's getting along," Bobby said suddenly. "It's tough getting the letters out, but I ain't heard from her since, I don't know when! Months. Seriously, months. I thought we was engaged, but you know."

"Oh don't start thinking that way," said Harry. "You'll get her thinking like that."

"Well, I ain't like you, Sly. I can't think about her. It makes me nuts," Bobby said. "I can't separate things."

"We're gonna have to deal with this mess for a long time," Sly said, "but now and then, a nice thought. Can't hurt."

"Yeah," Harry sat back down. "No harm in dreamin'"

Captain Harry Ashenbach and his men Sylvester Bapini and Bobby Pitro were lucky to be alive. Over the preceding 2 years, not a one of them had avoided life-threatening injuries. Yet, by November of 1944, they had been reunited in Italy, and there they were, working once again within the communications division of the US Army.

Harry's most recent catastrophe had found him and his small company more or less prisoners of geography. A sudden route away from safety in the middle of a moonless night had led to the calamitous tumbling into a deep, nearly inescapable rocky ravine. Mercifully, a small stream ran through which had made it possible for the company to survive that summer, having water and bits of food from the vegetation outcrops.

It was the bold but insistent demand of his compatriots, Sylvester and Bobby, that eventually led to the rescue of the entire company before any fatalities occurred.

That most recent adventure had tied the three souls together like brothers. While they were ranks apart in the military division, they were 100% equals in the human division.

At that moment, they were also 100% equally bored. The business of interrogating POWs had become quite familiar, and as such, less challenging. While it made the time pass, the men could not extinguish their recently developed thirst to be "in the fight."

"You perform a valid service," Harry's CO had said when Harry had requested transferring to a fighting division. "Remember, you were brought out from what amounted to retirement, Captain Ashenbach," he said. "The Army doesn't relish having its valuable instructors snuffed out for the sake of avoiding boredom.

"No, Sir," said Harry.

"If you had not agreed to help on those very vital missions, who knows what would have occurred? As it stands, we're struggling to meet our objectives, but you have to be satisfied with taking credit for the very important role you played in subverting Hitler."

It had been those words that had brought Harry to attention. Had he truly played a role in skewing something that madman was planning? His commander's words brought him health and he had tried to share that healing with the far younger Sylvester and Bobby, and the rest of his company.

But their relative youth and strength fought against it, feeling the natural urge to get back into the fight. Yet for the moment, they seemed to be able to satisfy themselves with discussing the work at hand and, of course, food.

"Well, you got that right," Sly was saying, "ain't a sandwich without at least the ham and salami."

"Capicola, you gotta have that. You don't have that, you can't taste the rest of it," Bobby argued.

"Okay, capicola's good, but it's the cheese that makes it taste good."

"Ah yeah, the cheese. You ever had that real strong provolone? Tastes like bleu almost."

"Yeah, and that's why I said the pickles, the olives and the pickles."

"Peppers. Don't forget them fried peppers in oil."

"And oregano."

"Yeah."

Harry shook his head. "What is this? The Army or Parchisi's Diner?"

"Hey where's that at?" asked Bobby. "Sounds like a good place."

Harry laughed. "I made it up."

"Oh." Bobby slumped back down. "I used to go to Rose's, you know, the corner there at 15th."

"I don't know Philly," said Sylvester. "But I bet they got some great food."

"Yeah, boy," Harry said. "I went to a convention once there, and it was full of good stops. That's where me and some guys made up our secret knock, you know, so we knew it was one of us."

"Secret knock," said Bobby. "How did it go?"

Harry knocked on a barometer, the only thing made of wood close by. "Like this," he said marking the off-beat rhythm.

"Hey that's good," said Sly. "We'll do that, too."

"Yeah," said Bobby. "If any of us visits another soggy tent, we can take this barometer with us."

Harry and Sly laughed. "But I like the idea," Sly said, and copied the funny knock.

"That's it," said Harry. "You got it."

"Let me try," said Bobby. "I'm a natural." And he was.

Just then a loud thunderclap sounded, followed by the arrival of a few gusts of wind, amidst the continuing series of daily downpours.

"Anyway, guess we ain't going to Philly today," Bobby said wryly. "Got a smoke?"

About 4500 miles away, it was much earlier in the day. St. Benedict's pastor, Father Bertrand stood in his living room. He replaced the receiver to his telephone. Deep in thought, he almost sat on his tiny white cat, now fully grown and queen of the rectory following his rescuing of her one year before.

"Oh, pardon me, little one!" he said scooping her up. One year old she was, but not much larger than the soaking, soiled ball of fur she had been as an abandoned kitten. She remained unperturbed, perfectly happy to rest on her benefactor's lap as long as he felt so inclined.

Father Bertrand stroked the little animal while traveling back in time to his moments with Great War wounded veterans. Counseling soldiers was not new to him. Following the earlier war years, there had been great strife and even uprisings because of the pain and abandonment the members of the military felt. In truth, they had not been appreciated as Father felt they should have been, and many had been left to linger in dire circumstances. Families were broken during that war, not only because of the many deaths it caused, but afterwards too, from alcoholism, depression, and even violence.

At that time, he and many of his fellow parish priests had determined that it would not happen again if they were to be involved in another war. The current war, he thought, as inevitable as it was with a madman in power, would produce even greater casualties. He had been prepared. But he had not been prepared for the suddenness of it. And not for the finality.

That morning, he had received a request for prayers for the repose of the soul of a severely burned veteran who had been treated at the hospital and counseled by another nearby priest. Somehow, the soldier had managed to get ahold of a full syringe of morphine and delivered it to his own vein. Whether his pain was so intense that he couldn't wait for the nurse and it was accidental, or his depression so great that he did not want to go on living, and it was intentional, no one knew. But the result either way was the loss of a man who had already sacrificed greatly.

His family would be devastated. Father Bertrand did not know them, nor would he be counseling them, but still their loss burned in his heart. Such a deep tragedy happening, just when they had hope that he would come home to them.

Just then, he heard a knock on the door. Kitty was up, looking around the room. She had come to know that her cozy resting spot would be interrupted following that familiar sound.

Father smiled and placed her back onto the chair as he stood. "Well, at least it's warmed up for you," he said out loud.

Father opened the door to a smiling Helen Ashenbach. "I hope I'm not interrupting, Father," she said. "But just in case, I've brought these honey biscuits to make up for it."

"You're never an interruption, Mrs. Ashenbach," Father said. "But I hope that doesn't mean I don't get the goodies?"

Helen laughed and stepped inside. "Oh it's cozy and warm in here. Hello, Kitty. She's so sweet," she said, stroking the little animal. "You're lucky to have such good company. I should have a pet, maybe."

"She is good company, and she sometimes thinks she's a watchdog. Don't you, Kitty? Please," he motioned to Helen, "have a seat."

"Thank you," said Helen. "I won't stay long. But I felt I needed to see you about a fellow who's in the hospital there in Atlantic City."

Father was startled. News traveled, he thought. "You don't mean the young man who died this morning?"

"Died! Oh good heavens, I hope not! You don't mean Bob McGarrett!"

"No, no, this was another fellow," Father said quickly. "I'm sorry. I jumped to a conclusion."

"I'm so sorry," said Helen. "Did you lose a . . . someone?"

"I was simply asked for prayers," he answered. "This young man was in the burn room, and in great pain."

"It was merciful then," said Helen, making the sign of the Cross.

"Yes," said Father, hopefully. "Who is Bob McGarrett?"

After Helen had explained, Father was enthused and resolved to visit Bob immediately. "Usually Monsignor Kuchesky visits the soldiers, and all of those in the hospitals," he said. "But knowing this young man is part of our extended family, I'd like to see him, too."

"Thank you so much. I think he will come around, especially with your help. He's had a rough time of it and there is definitely something bothering him other than just his injury. In fact, I don't think that's on his mind at all!"

"Sounds like a deeply sensitive person."

"Yes, Father, I think he is, and of course like all the men, has become more so with this awful war."

"I appreciate your telling me about him," Father said. "With or without the honey biscuits!"

Chapter Four

As the days grew shorter and far colder, conserving heating fuel by lighting fires grew popular. Helen's home was the favorite spot to congregate, but Joan's grade school friend Laureen, who lived in the neighborhood with her mother, also had a cozy fireplace room.

"Come on over," Laureen told Joan that morning. "I'll make us some lunch and we can catch up by the fire."

"And talk about Dick and Bob?" Joan giggled. It seemed that they had grown closer since both of their fiancés had been deployed. Laureen had been the shoulder for Joan to cry on more than once over the months, reassuring and kind.

When Joan had learned of Dick's injury, she'd nearly come apart with the fear, pain, sorrow and helplessness. Annie had been there, with Helen and Bernice, but so had Laureen, always reminding her that things looked and sounded worse at a distance. She suggested Joan keep the good thought and try to figure out how Dick would want her to act.

The bond would have been even stronger between the five of them had it not been for the fact that Laureen was not as available, still happily employed full time.

It was on her day off that Laureen got to stay at home and asked Joan over for lunch.

Nervously she worked at the sandwiches, spreading the salad dressing, arranging the pickles and cheese, then trimming off the crusts. Laureen was not an open person to begin with. While she loved to share comfort and listen to friends' problems, she tended to hold her own feelings "close to the vest," as Bob would say. Bob. Laureen nearly broke down for the third time that day, but managed to avoid it by thinking about how many pints in a quart, how many quarts in a gallon, so how many pints in a gallon.

It was absurd, but she had taught herself such little distractions over the years to avoid spilling her guts whenever she felt something overwhelming. That day, she was nervous. She loved Joan, and she knew that she had been a bastion of strength for Joan, who was frequently emotional. What would happen if Laureen could not contain herself, her emotions? Everyone said *not knowing* was the worst thing. But that wasn't quite right. Sometimes actually knowing was the worst.

Laureen arranged the sandwiches on a pretty sandwich platter on which a colorful, three-dimensional figure of a milk maid with a pail stood smiling in the center. She then sliced some carrots and decorated the center with them and took the plate into the cozy fireplace room.

The warmth of the room, and its memories of happier times warmed her heart and gave her hope.

She wouldn't break down in front of Joan. There was no reason to worry about that. Situations like these came up in life, and she was strong enough, she told herself, experienced enough to manage without burdening others with emotional outbursts. How many pints in a gallon?

She checked her appearance in the hall mirror. Her golden hair was arranged in a gentle updo with a soft roll that reached her shoulder blades. Laureen rarely had to worry about her hair. The thick, smooth look of spun gold was hereditary, and despite her denials, it was the envy of many of the Abbottsville women. Unless she was out with Bob, though, Laureen tended to keep it under wraps, which no doubt contributed to its overall health.

She wore a dark green cardigan over a simple white blouse, and a single strand of pearls. Her skirt was a green plaid the color of ivy, with black and grey shades mixed in.

She sighed, resolving once more that she was a strong and capable young woman, just having a visit with a friend. No histrionics.

The doorbell rang.

Joan had come on foot, which was not at all unusual, as riding in a car the five or six blocks in those days would have been laughed at. The only buses ran down the main street, which would have meant walking to 23rd, catching a bus for a block, then getting off and walking down four more blocks. That didn't make sense, Joan decided. Annie had agreed at dinner the night before.

"That's why you got the job at J. C. Penny," she'd said, "you've got brains."

Joan sighed. Her sarcastic best friend did not miss a trick. Annie had gone off to work at the same time Joan had left the house, but they'd taken different routes.

"Golly! Dress for that crazy wind," Joan had warned her as she stepped out the door. Then she giggled as Annie's hat had flown right back into the house. Annie reappeared, her hair blown around like a wild woman's, grabbed her hat, stuck her tongue out at Joan and exited again.

The wind never seemed to settle once it got started in October or November. Joan took a scarf and hat for her journey and made sure it was secure before she opened the door to the outside. She was happy that she'd been prudent about that, but the pleated skirt and thin sweater she'd picked out left her looking forward very much to that cozy fire Laureen had described.

She stood waiting for her friend to open the door, remembering how kind Laureen had always been. One of these days, she told herself, I would like to be there for Laureen instead of always the other way around.

Laureen opened the door, looked into the warm, happy eyes of her friend, threw her arms around her and abruptly burst into tears.

Further into the city, Helen tried to read her magazine as the bus jiggled and joggled down its bumpy course on the broken streets.

"Feels like they been shelling!" said a woman across from her.

Helen smiled. She had thought the same thing. Bumps and pot holes in the road could not be repaired due to scarcity of materials. Nevertheless, she was glad to be inside. For once, she wished the bus trip from Atlantic City to Abbotsville were longer. She needed to think over the conversation she'd had with Bob at the hospital, try to form the best response, the best sort of plan or answer for Laureen.

The nurse told her Bob was due to be transferred back to his hometown, Washington, D.C. "We've done all we can for him here," she had explained. "His body is starting to heal, and so far, he's kept the leg, but his mind is the problem. I have seen men depressed before, but this fellow won't even talk!"

Helen knew that to be true from her previous visit. He had talked, but only a few words, and they had not been very enlightening.

But her visit on that particular day had been quite different. Bob had been positioned in a wheelchair to face a window. She approached from behind him, calling his name so that he might recognize her voice before turning around to see her. She wasn't sure whether he could maneuver on his own yet or not.

"Go," he had said, waving his hand. "I don't need any lunch, I don't need anything."

But Helen was no stranger to obstinance. "Well I didn't bring you any lunch," she said turning him to face her, "and if I had, I wouldn't give it to you now!" She said it with a twinkle in her eye.

When Bob saw who it was, he lowered his head. "I'm sorry Mrs. Ashenbach."

"Let's go back to your place so we can talk."

"Yeah, my place," he said roughly.

Once they were situated with the curtain containing their conversation a little bit, Helen said plainly, "Bob, I understand that you're facing a challenge. But I don't understand your mistreatment of your family and that dear girl, Laureen. I gave her the news about you, and she has tried to see you several times and you refuse. Why are you doing that?"

Bob shook his head. "You say you understand, Mrs. Ashenbach, but you couldn't possibly."

Helen said nothing. She was prepared for his response.

"I mean that," he said. "You are coming at this from one place, and me, I'm in a world away, an entire world history away."

"Yes, you are," said Helen.

"There's things, crap, sorry, but stuff you won't ever hopefully see or know about. I was there to try to change that, to make sure, to help get them guys, to help. . ."

Bob seemed to go into a daze at that point, his mind drifting. Helen knew it was partly the medicine, partly the reverie of things she would never know of, first-hand, anyway. "Bob," she said gently, "you're right. I don't know about those things. I don't think I will ever know about them. But I know the longing you must feel, and depression and despair as well, to have been separated from that, from your men, your. . ." She searched for the word Harry had used those many years before. "Brothers," she said finally.

Her words seemed to have had an impact. He looked up at her, and for a moment, she could see in his eyes, the warm gentle look of the Bob who had come to the Christmas Dance with Laureen; the happy couple newly engaged with only a happy future to ponder and dream about. But it was only a flash. Bob looked down again, focusing on the bandage at his knee.

Helen knew that she had reached him, if only for a second. But she was wise enough to know not to push. It was a special language she used, and that language required a great deal more listening than speech. She waited.

It was some time before Bob moved again. It seemed as if he was going to tell her to leave. His once broad proud shoulders slumped, but she could see that they were still strong. There was no question that his body was injured, but it was his mind that needed healing. And unlike the treatment of his leg, healing of his mind would require his permission, his sanctioning.

He raised his head and put out his hand. It was tentative, and it trembled, but it was sure. Helen took it. "I need. . ." he said.

"Yes," said Helen. Bob didn't see her smile as he lowered his head to conceal a tear, but to Helen, Heaven had just opened and sent down a shaft of brilliant light upon them.

"May I come back?" Helen asked as she stood to go.

"Yes," said Bob, with less hesitation than before.

"May I bring Laureen?" Helen asked quietly.

Bob exhaled slowly. "Yes, but. . . not yet."

Chapter Five

"Oh Annie," said Joan sadly, "my heart was breaking for her. I've never seen Laureen like that."

"Poor girl. She might be strong, but she's just as vulnerable as you or I. I guess everyone's got a breaking point," said Annie.

"Soup is ready!" Helen called from the kitchen. She carried in a tray with the four bowls of the soup that she and Bernice had made earlier. "Fresh and hot from the Ashenbach-St. John Kitchens!"

Bernice brought in the pitcher of milk. "Hope you like it!" she said, taking a seat.

"It smells heavenly," Joan said. "You are really getting into the cooking thing, huh Bernice?"

"I'm learning tons about the grocery business," Bernice said. "One of the big things is there's a market value for all groceries. Fresh vegetables are one of the ones that has a pretty short shelf life, as they call it. So there are those who will benefit from that, including us!"

"Okay by me," said Annie.

After Grace was said and the girls were enjoying their light dinner, Helen spoke. "It's very sad what

Laureen is going through. I feel terrible for her. But please try to avoid being angry with Bob. His life right now is completely turned around."

"I can understand that he's in pain," Joan said, "and that he's worried about his leg. But that's no reason to snub Laureen. She's really hurting."

The other girls were quiet, reflecting on their feelings. It all seemed so unreal. Laureen and Bob had been Laureen and Bob before any of the other couples had been engaged. They were happy, secure, always the ones to depend on, to go to for help. Laureen had helped Joan get to know Dick, and Bob had been Dick's buddy, even before the service, helping him navigate the world of women, as well as could be done. The two of them had helped with all of the dances, always a shining example of true love. And now this.

"Did he mention anything about, well, you know, calling it off?" Bernice said wincing. "I would just hate to hear that."

"So would I," said Annie. She could not force herself to imagine what it would feel like. The idea of her man surviving the war, being home for good, and then having him reject her. It was too much. She drew in her breath sharply.

"You okay?" Joan asked. "What was that?"

"That was me imagining it was me and Sylvester going through this. I couldn't take it. I just couldn't." She closed her eyes and sighed. What a dark and hopeless world that would be, she thought.

"Well, girls, that's what I'm trying to say. I don't think it will turn out that way. But remember, Bob has been through times that we may never come to understand. He feels like he's not Bob, or at least not with the personality he had before," Helen said. "He needs time to try to bridge that gap between the parts of the old Bob and the newly injured Bob that he is right now."

"But Helen, how can getting a leg wound make a person change that much? Laureen said to me that until you told her about him, she didn't even know where he was. That's not right," said Joan.

Helen nodded. "Yes, I know how you feel. But you're not looking at this in the context of the War. If Bob had gone away on a vacation and returned acting like this, I think your reaction would be appropriate. But girls, he fought in a war. That's not the same thing as reading about it or even losing someone to it. It's being there, seeing and hearing things, smelling things, fears that you never imagined you would have to live through. Dark, brutal things like the violent death of a comrade, right beside you.

"And that's not all. On top of that, poor Bob feels the full weight of guilt."

"Guilt?" said Annie. "Guilt about what?"

"I think I know," said Bernice.

"What?" Joan asked. "What did he do?"

"I don't think it's actually what he *did*," Bernice answered.

"No, it isn't, you're right Bernice. Remember, Joan, he was with Dick all the way through it. They supported each other. Apparently Dick led the men on a very dangerous exploratory mission and Bob was with him when he was hurt."

"So why does he feel guilty?"

"Because he's not there anymore," said Bernice. "He's letting Dick and the others down."

"That's it exactly," said Helen. "These guys aren't thinking that it's all about them. They're thinking what was drilled into them at training—I have to take care of my buddy. So in his mind, he's letting the guys down. Well, how can he support them all the way back home here?

Annie leaned back and sighed. "They didn't seem like that at Christmas. They were all going back, though, still together, still like a team. Maybe those feelings aren't for us to know about. Or maybe they hadn't had as bad of an experience by then. Of course Bob and Dick were still stateside, hadn't been in the action, as Sylvester calls it."

"It's true that some of the men are posted behind the lines, out of range of the actual conflict, like the linguists and some of the other groups. And maybe that's why we didn't have the same situation," Helen said, "but remember, Harry was in the first war to end all wars. This is not new to him. We've had our share of this."

"Oh Helen," said Joan, touching her shoulder.

"It was no picnic, I'll tell you that," Helen continued. "And now that most of these fellows have seen battle, you will have to try to get ahold of your emotions. It's not going to be easy for them. They'll need your support in ways that are new to both of you."

As the radio played the soft sounds of vocal groups, and the four women cleaned up after dinner, Bernice spoke up.   "Speaking of guys coming home," she said, holding up a letter. "I got this from Henry today."

"Henry? My goodness, how is he?" asked Helen.

"He sounds just like the old Henry," said Bernice. "Of course, he's always been good at making things casual."

"Is he one of those stoic kinds?" asked Annie. "Pretends nothing affects him, and then all of the sudden pow! He's on his feet! That kind of guy?"

"No, but he *is* low key," Bernice said. "He likes to keep a low profile, keep things easy, uncomplicated."

"He sounds nice," Annie said smiling. "I never really got to know him."

"Well you might yet," said Bernice. "It looks like he's going to be discharged, or is already discharged on a medical. He'll actually be at home with outpatient orders to the Thomas England Veteran's."

Joan sat back down at the table and poured herself another glass of milk. "How do you feel about that, Bernice? Him being back here and all?"

"Happy," Bernice said without hesitation. "I'm happy he survived, happy he is coming home, and I'll be happy to get him to and from the hospital as need be."

Joan smiled. Bernice was a beautiful open book, she thought. Her romance with Henry had wound down, but she still cared for him. It was lucky for Henry. Not everyone had such a little spitfire looking out for them.

"You're gooder than me," Annie said.

"Oh shut up," said Bernice. "You're just jealous because I have a man to look out for."

"You got that right," said Annie.

"Hey, I wasn't serious," Bernice said. "I didn't mean to hurt your feelings!"

"It's all right!" Annie said quickly. "But you are right. And I might even horn in on your nursey routine. He'll have two of us fawning all over him."

"Make that three—or four!" Helen chimed in. "We want in, too!" She elbowed Joan, who giggled.

"Yeah! When is he due in?" Joan asked.

"I couldn't tell from this letter," Bernice answered. "But I think they were ready to get him out of there when he wrote. It could be any day."

"He's probably counting the days," said Annie, pretending to swoon.

"Yeah, you know it ain't like that."

"Seriously Bernice," Annie said softly, "I hope he's okay, you know, after everything he's been through."

"Me, too," said Bernice smiling.

"I hate to bring up another troubling subject," said Annie, "but Margaret's on the lookout again."

"On the lookout?" Helen said. "What do you mean? For what?"

"Probably a *who*," said Joan wryly. "Right, Annie?"

"Actually yes. She's willing to forget Bernice's interference and go for the gusto one more time."

"My *what*? Interference?" Bernice was on her feet. "What do you mean?"

Annie laughed. "Don't you remember? She was sure that you had stolen her boyfriend. Of course her sense of logic never played into it because she has never explained how it is that you are not dating anyone. So how could it be that you stole him away from her?"

"Maybe she thinks I got him in a cage at home," Bernice said, looking for her glass. "Did you wash everything already, Helen?"

"Ask Joan. She's the dishwasher."

"Yep," said Joan without any sympathy.

"Thanks a lot. I notice *you* still have a glass, and milk, too."

"You snooze, you lose," said Joan, shaking her head like a mother.

"I think you ought to give Henry to Margaret," said Annie. "Then you'd be even for stealing hers. It's the least you could do."

"I'm thinking she might have a taste for that big Italian of yours," Bernice answered.

"Okay ladies, enough of this banter," said Helen, dropping a heavy binder onto the freshly cleared table. "Let's get down to the plans we need to make. Time's a'wastin'!"

Chapter Six

The winter sky was black except for the golden streams of reflected light from the full moon. Not even a tiny glow of light could be seen throughout the neighborhood. Yet all around were homes filled with people doing everyday things; fires burned in the parlor fireplaces, trash was gathered and stored in paper bags and set in metal cans outside, and children sat by radios, waiting to hear their nighttime programs.

At 6 North Edison, the girls were just finishing up plans for the Christmas Bazaar.

Annie moved to the heavily blacked out window. "I'll be glad when we can look at the stars again," she said, wanting madly to move the heavy fabric even just a little.

Helen joined her. "Me, too," she said. "When I start feeling that way, though, I think about London."

"Yeah," said Bernice. "Or Poland, or Lithuania."

"Do you want me to sweep in here?" Joan asked as she gathered the notes together on the table.

"No, that's fine, Honey," Helen said.

"They've still got rocket attacks in London, don't they," said Annie. "Even though they're giving it to the Germans good now."

"Yeah," said Joan. "I read they've got V8s over there now."

Annie burst out laughing. "Yeah, V8s," she said. "They just take them big cans and throw real hard."

Helen tried to hide a smile, not wanting to offend Joan. But Bernice wasn't worried.

"Yeah, if they burst, everybody's covered in vegetable juice, and boy that's embarrassing."

"What a way to win a war, huh Joanie?"

Joan put down the papers. She was chuckling but still trying to come up with the right word. "Well, what was it that I heard? V rockets or something?"

"Yes," Helen said, "you just had the wrong number."

"And beverage," added Bernice.

"They're V2s," Annie said.

"Well, I was only 6 off," said Joan, sticking her tongue out at Annie.

"Yeah Annie," said Bernice. "And personally, I'd rather have one of Joan's vegetable bombs than your Nazi one."

"Who wants coffee?" Helen said chuckling and shaking her head. "I got my ration today and I'm happy to share!"

"Count me in!" called Annie.

Bernice and Joan looked at each other. "We'll all have some," said Joan, "unless you guys would rather have a glass of V8?"

They gathered in the living room once the coffee was served.

"This is heavenly," Annie said, choosing the arm of the sofa to sit on. "You really know how to make a cup of coffee, Helen."

"You got that right," said Bernice. "I never drank coffee until all this started, you know, the war and all."

Helen nodded. "I guess some folks started in with other beverages, but frankly, I think coffee's just as nice and you don't have to worry about getting sick or overdoing it. And I like it any time of day."

Joan sighed. "Me, too. Gosh, we sound like the Luzianne Coffee commercial!" She laughed. "Think they'll take us on?"

"We'll have to come up with a little song," Helen said smiling. "You can do that part, Bernice."

The four sat quietly for a while, feeling the warmth of their friendships and peace of the moment. "It's sure nice to, you know, be around you all," said Joan tentatively. "It's kind of a cozy feeling, a protective feeling."

"I know what you mean," Annie said. "It feels like a separate family or something."

"I don't know what I would have done last year this time, remember?"

Bernice giggled. "That redhead. What was her name?"

"Gloria," Joan shot back. "Oh, sorry. I didn't mean to say that with such force!" She blushed.

"Gloria Marini," said Annie. "Oh yes. I wonder what she's up to now."

"Chances are she's still setting traps for Dick!" Bernice said.

Everyone giggled. Except for Joan. "I wonder if she is," she said thoughtfully.

"I was only kidding you," said Bernice. "He's not even here!"

"I know, but, well, I guess it's starting to get to me," said Joan. "It's been quite a while since he wrote. And who knows, maybe he's somewhere else. Maybe he got well and decided to spend the rest of the war in France or something."

"Yeah, you mean he picked himself up a floozy?" Annie said. "Now, when I say it, don't it sound silly?"

Joan smiled, remembering Annie's suspicions of her Sylvester at right around the same time the year before. "Well what do you think is happening?" she persisted. "There's no viable reason why he wouldn't have written if he were still interested."

"Still interested?" Helen asked. "You're engaged aren't you, Honey? How much more interested could he be, short of marrying you long distance? And I don't think anybody wants that!"

"You're right, you're right," said Joan. "Well, what do you think I should do? Just kind of sit it out, and not write for a while, and see what happens?"

"I would," said Annie. "But not in an angry way, just kind of give him your understanding. He's already proposed, so you know what he feels. But if he's in a place where he can't write or if they've got him moving around, traveling, I'm sure he'll really appreciate your patience."

"I think that's the perfect advice," said Helen.

"Well," Bernice said, "you could write, but just be encouraging and upbeat. You know, tell him what good stuff is going on, what you made for dinner, how things are going with the bazaar, share some memories, that kind of thing. Don't ask him why he's not writing or if there's some kind of problem. Give him a little latitude but let him know you're still behind him."

Helen nodded. "That's a good idea, too," she agreed. "But I wouldn't set your hopes high that as soon as you send out that letter he'll shoot one out in the mail right away."

"Helen could be right," Bernice said. "After all, I'm the one who's supposed to be thinking about becoming a nun. What do I know anyway?"

"Thinking about?" Annie said. "What do you mean, 'thinking about'?"

"Well, discerning I guess is the word," said Bernice.

Annie and Helen exchanged glances.

"Thanks you guys," said Joan obliviously. "Just like I said, it's like having a second family with you all."

That night, when Annie and Joan walked home together, Annie was uncharacteristically quiet.

"You okay, Annie?" Joan asked. Her friend was usually in charge of three-quarters of the conversation. "You're awfully quiet."

"I'm okay, I guess," Annie said.

They walked on in silence. But just after they entered their home, Annie burst out, "Oh why do people gotta be so mean to each other?"

Indivisible-Cece Whittaker

Startled, Joan dropped her pocketbook. Reaching down to pick it up, she looked up at Annie, who was keenly unhappy. Her mouth was turned down at the corners, and she looked as if she were about to cry. "Oh Annie, I don't know," she said, reaching out to hug her. "Is there something special bothering you? Who's being mean to you?"

"No, no," Annie answered, instantly repentant for having let loose such a fury of emotion. "No, forget it, Joanie. I'm just having one of those blue kind of days."

"Were you talking about the way Bob hasn't contacted Laureen? I know that's not very nice, but as Helen said, there could be more than we know, way more, where the only eyes who know the whole story are watching from Heaven," Joan said. "Here, let me have your coat. I'll put it up and then we can maybe have a fire. Okay?"

"Yeah, that sounds nice," Annie said, handing her coat over to Joan gently, patting it, as if trying to comfort it. Softly, she continued, "There's a war on for crying out loud. We got enough trouble already." Then she started to cry.

Okay, this is not about Bob, Joan thought, and it's not about the War, although either one of those things would be enough. This whole separation from and unknowing about Sylvester's whereabouts was really beginning to take its toll on poor Annie.

The luster in her friend's eyes had dimmed considerably, despite all of Annie's efforts to remain positive. It seemed that she was collapsing before Joan's very eyes.

"Oh Annie, I'm so sorry. I've been thinking about my own problems so much, I haven't realized how much this uncertainty has been hurting you." Joan wrapped her arms around Annie, trying to keep from crying herself.

Annie hugged her back, then straightened up, wiped her eyes, and said, "Thanks Joanie. You're always there for me." She picked up an afghan and cozied herself on the couch, snuggling in like a child. "It's not just missing Sylvester, and Dear God, I do," she began. "I am also missing being somebody's girl. I heard a man laugh the other day, and it sounded like Sly's laugh. It made me want to just go to sleep 'til it's all over.

"He wasn't here that long, so it doesn't make sense," Annie continued, staring at the black window treatment. "But Joanie, even though I seem strong and independent, I really need to be with him, belong to him, not just the shadow of him." Suddenly she sat forward and pounded her fist onto her knee, the tears returning, "And I need to know where he is!"

Chapter Seven

"Well, good morning!" said a buxom, cheerful volunteer as she opened the curtains in Dick Thimble's room. "It sure is nice to see the whites of your eyes!" She giggled at her own joke as she picked up a tray of breakfast, its contents rattling as she set them down ungently on a table next to Dick. "You been sleeping a long time. Doc says to get some food in you before you perish. Can ya eat?"

The room was unfamiliar, as was the volunteer. Dick had a vague recollection of being carted onto a plane, but only bits and pieces of memory chased each other around in his brain beyond that. The woman's loud, country-tinted voice was welcome, but somehow assaulting at the same time.

He opened his mouth to speak. That's when he realized how thirsty he was. The juice on her tray looked good, and so did the coffee.

He tried to sit up. Immediately the woman was at his elbow. "Oh no Honey, don't you try and set up, you been on your back fer a long time. You gotta lemme hep ya." She put one fleshy but muscular arm behind him, and the other under his near arm pit and lifted him up as easily as taking bread out of the toaster. "That don't hurt, now, do it?" she asked, looking at him carefully in the face. "I been trained on how to handle emaciated folks, so I think I done it right."

Emaciated! Did she say *emaciated?* Dick reached for the juice, but again she intercepted. "Here you go, Honey," she said. "I'll hold onto it, you use this here straw."

Dick obeyed. As the stream of orange juice rolled over his parched tongue, he immediately felt a rush of energy and a great burst of goodwill. He knew he was in a good place, and he was happy and excited to be alive, wherever he was. He took another sip which sent him into a wild coughing spell and quickly brought him back down to earth.

The woman patted him on the back. "Take it easy, there. That's good stuff, fortified with Vitamin C, you know, keeps your bones strong and straight, but you gotta go easy at first. Little sips, Honey."

Dick complied, and slowly brought his consciousness forward into the world. Once he felt he could talk, he asked, "Where am I?"

The volunteer threw back her head and laughed heartily. "You wouldn't believe how many times I hear that question," she said, taking a seat next to him. She wasn't an ugly woman, just a little overstuffed, Dick decided. And she had a warmth about her that anyone being treated would surely appreciate.

"You're at Mercy Hospital," she said. "You come in here the beginning of November, from overseas they tell me."

"Near Fort Sill?" Dick said, his voice hoarse.

"Yep, Oklahoma," she said proudly. "The story I got is you had a gunshot wound went bad. That happens a lot at them camps. We had one fellow lost his foot because of it. Sad, sad. But you ain't gonna lose nothin'," she said merrily. "Your injury was in the buttock, and I think you're gonna keep both of those."

Dick smiled, thinking how funny it would be to have to go through life with only one buttock. And after his exhausting morning, he fell into a sound sleep.

He woke to the ticking sound of a clock echoing through the hall. Amazed at how similar it was to his father's clock at home, he decided to investigate. As he approached it, he realized that it was very, very foggy in the house. It must be humidity from the creek, he thought. Someone has left the door open.

At the open door, he stepped outside, onto the porch. That's funny, he thought, this porch is in really bad shape. Dad must be too busy to keep it up. There's dirt everywhere.

But it wasn't the porch actually. It was a sliver of ground high on a ridge along the coast of France. Grateful that he hadn't come out of the house at high speed, Dick struggled to keep his balance, crossing the long narrow strip. This is the first time I've used this technique since training, he thought, balancing remarkably well to the point of floating over holes in the terrain at times.

Finally, he reached the other side but was instantly filled with regret. There were men on the ground beyond, moaning. A wind had aroused with icy cold fingers, circling his arms and legs, making it harder and harder to move. He heard the sounds of moans growing closer. They must be wounded, he thought. Let me find some blankets. There must be supplies around here some place.

Suddenly amongst the men, he spotted Bob. "Bob," he called out. Bob looked up at him. He was ashen, his leg horribly wounded. I've got my coat, Dick thought. I could give him that.

"Hang on," he said, "I'm coming." But Bob was fading, his arms and legs wavering into nothing. "Hold on!" Dick repeated. "I'm coming!"

But the more Dick tried to move, the heavier his hands and feet felt, as if they were sinking into quicksand. "Bob!" he cried out. "Bob, I'm coming!"

Just then he freed his hand so violently that he knocked himself down to the ground. It was such a hard ground, cold, and steely, and so desolate.

Suddenly a light came on and he realized his eyes had been closed. He was looking at the steel grey legs of a bed on a black and white tiled floor. His body hunched forward, and he threw up.

Abruptly there was activity. Shoes and then pairs of arms all around him.

"Dear God," said a frantic voice. "He's burning up. That plasma must have been contaminated. Call the doctor! Hang on Richard, stay with us!"

And then, as he was lifted back onto his bed, a slow darkness rolled across and over him. As the emergency charged atmosphere gently faded away, he fell into a complacent near-death sleep.

Chapter Eight

Laureen sat on the Pacific Avenue bus. As she stared into the cold grey afternoon, she could hear her mother still warning her. "If he doesn't call you, he doesn't want to see you yet. He will get in touch with you when the time is right. If you go on ahead and barge in, you may cause a lot of trouble, Laureen. I don't think you will like how it ends up."

The bus was chilly, and she shivered. Her heartbeat raced as they rolled closer to the hospital. Passing the last few cross streets, she almost decided to turn back. It could have been curiosity, loneliness, or a misplaced sense of loyalty, but something urged her on. I'll be cheerful and kind, she told herself. That's all he needs, just to see me, and remember the old times. It hasn't even been a year. What could happen in that time?

An older gentleman grasping a cane seemed to understand her anxiety. "Visiting your sweetheart?" he asked as they got up to exit the bus.

Not knowing how to answer, Laureen smiled and simply nodded.

"It's the best thing for 'em," the man said. "Good old-fashioned love and devotion. That'll heal 'em up quicker every time."

"Thank you," said Laureen, still smiling. But as the man advanced awkwardly toward the building, her smile faded. "What if he won't see me?" she said softly.

Inside, it was warm, and the light was welcoming. Some of her friends were nervous to go where the soldiers were located. They feared that the presence of soldiers would draw the attention of and maybe attacks from the Nazis. There certainly were an abundance of soldiers! She looked out toward the beach and caught sight of a marching unit, followed by a second, and then a third.

Although the wind was whipping through her scarf, she stood and watched, fascinated. How beautiful they look, she thought. Not only how they look but what they are, what they will do just to keep me and all of us safe. Tears gathered in her eyes, hotly blurring her reasons for coming. Her heart was literally aching to be with Bob. Even if she couldn't hold him, just to see him, touch his hand, that would be all right.

"But he doesn't want me!" she wept out loud, then quickly aware of her circumstances, wiped her eyes and followed the sidewalk into the front doors of the hospital.

At the reception area, Laureen was startled to see fully uniformed soldiers, one on either side of the desk. Again, she took herself to task. What was I thinking? That I would just waltz right in and go wherever I wanted?

As if reading her mind, the nurse at the desk put her hand up slightly, and said, "This is a military hospital, Miss. You will need an escort to go any further."

"An . . . escort?" Laureen stammered.

"Yes. Who are you here to see?"

"I want to see Robert McGarrett."

"McGarrett. . . McGarrett. . .oh, okay, I know. Is he with Father Bertrand of Abbotsville this afternoon?" she asked one of the guards.

He shrugged.

"Oh, yes, I, uh, I work for Father Bertrand," lied Laureen. "I need to see him."

"Okay," said the nurse. "Go ahead."

Laureen started but then stopped. "I'm sorry, what room is that?"

"Don't worry, Private Gussop will escort you. But if you're with Father when you leave, you won't need an escort."

Private Gussop was tall and handsome and took his assignment most seriously. "Follow me, Miss," he said.

They traveled up some floors and down a long hall. When they got to the end, a patient was being moved on a stretcher, which temporarily blocked their way.

"His room is the next one," Gussop said. "It's the last room on this hallway. Is it all right if I leave you here? I don't like to leave my post for too long, and it looks like these folks are going to be a while."

"No, please, go ahead," said Laureen. But even after the hall was completely clear, Laureen stood, moving neither forward nor backward. After a while, afraid someone might see her and think she was a misplaced mental patient, she moved a little further down the hall. About ten paces outside of that last room, there were a couple of chairs situated up against the wall.

Just as she had sat down, she heard a beloved and familiar voice. Bob, she thought, catching her breath. What was he saying, something. . . She could not make it out. Since no one was on the floor, she decided it might be more advantageous to take the closer chair. In sitting down, she failed to notice that the pocketbook on her arm was upside down. Most of its contents clanked noisily onto the polished hospital tiled floor.

The voice in the room came to an abrupt stop and Laureen froze halfway to the chair, again looking somewhat like an *avant gard* statue. She looked around but saw nobody emerging from any of the rooms. Providentially Bob's voice resumed. As silently as possible, Laureen scooped up her belongings and replaced them in her purse.

She moved to the chair furthest down and found that she could hear much better there. Bob was explaining something about the geography of France to someone. Then she heard another voice. It was male. That must be Father, she thought.

"Believe it or not, I think I have spoken with another soldier who was in that same location," he was saying. "Quite a few remained in that area after the big invasion."

"I didn't get this," Bob said, "during any invasion."

"It looks like it's coming along," said Father. "I expect it won't be long before they have you walking on it."

"Already have, with a set of crutches," Bob seemed to growl.

"I take it things have been a little rough," Father said.

Bob was quiet for a while. "Father, I am having trouble dealing with this," he said, "but right now I'm really—"

Laureen was startled by the sudden appearance of a nun in apparently silent shoes approaching. She smiled at Laureen and continued on to Bob's room.

"Time for a pill Sergeant McGarrett," she said.

Sergeant? Laureen thought he was *Private* McGarrett.

Apparently Bob took the pill because no one spoke for a moment. But then he picked up again. "Thank you, Sister. Father, I might as well tell you, I'm in a very deep depression. I feel guiltier than I ever have."

"Guilty?" said Father. "Surely—"

"Not the regular kind of guilty," Bob interrupted. "Guilty because a friend of mine is in such terrible shape."

"That's understandable," Father said.

"You probably don't know Dick Thimble," Bob went on.

Laureen's ears pricked up and she moved forward in her chair.

"He's in terrible shape. He was shot, and we all thought ha ha, real funny because it happened to be, well, he got shot in the ass, Father. Oh, sorry Sister!"

The nun giggled. "No harm done, Robert."

"We all made this big joke, and if you know Dick, you know he played along. Well something happened, and by the time we got to London, he was really in bad shape. He had a boiling hot fever from some infection or something. He was half out of his head. Couldn't keep anything down, and the guys there couldn't do anything with him. By the time I shipped out to come here, he wasn't even conscious. The last I heard, he was supposed to be coming, too, but I haven't seen him. I'm sick about it." Bob paused for a moment, and Laureen thought she heard a sob. "I'm afraid he might be dead."

Laureen froze. Her mind went instantly to her dear friend Joan. As far as Joan knew, Dick had just decided to stop writing for a while; that he was stationed in Oklahoma and that was that. Even with her emotions already taut, Laureen's heart was breaking for Joan.

"Oh what do I do?" she whispered out loud, startling herself. Poor Joanie—should I tell her? Maybe something good has happened and he's getting well now. But what if. . . oh that just can't be. If it were me, I would want to know. I think.

She could hear the conversation picking up again in Bob's room, but she knew at that point that seeing Bob would not be right. Not only had he said he wanted to wait until he was ready, she would have Dick's fate, and Joanie's whole world so heavily on her mind that she couldn't possibly be composed and share her heart with him. In fact, she thought, it could be downright disastrous.

She grabbed her purse—right side up—and scurried down the hall and out to the return bus home.

At Helen's house, the radio played soft music to the rhythm of Helen's iron on the ironing board. Steam hissed as the hot metal joined with the moistened cotton blouse, sending up smoke tendrils like journeys into the past.

A Tommy Dorsey number played, and Helen set the iron down, and grabbed a hanger, swaying to the music as she did so. In her crystal memory, she could see Harry's hand on her shoulder, hear his soft laughter as they danced and joked around, right there in that very living room.

She sighed, putting the blouse neatly onto the hanger. She surveyed her work. Isn't it nice how once you finish the ironing, the colors and the pattern look so much prettier, she thought. Even plain white looks nicer when it's freshly ironed.

She hooked the top of the hanger on the arm of a dining room chair and returned to her bag of wash. Just then she heard the familiar scuff of shoes on the welcome mat, followed by the tap tap tap on her front door, as it opened.

"It's got to be Bernice," she called out cheerily. "Who else knocks on the door and comes in at the same time?"

Bernice stood in the doorway. "You're right," she said. She stepped outside and closed the door. And after a moment's pause, she knocked.

Helen giggled and went to the door. "Very funny, Bernice," she said. "Come in. I'm doing a little wash. You want a cup of tea?"

"Yeah, thanks, I'll get it and then join you," Bernice answered heading for the kitchen. "Wait 'til you find out my news!"

Helen followed her in. "I'll hear it now, thank you!" she said.

Smiling, Bernice said, "Guess who's getting in this afternoon?"

"Henry!"

"Yes!"

"My stars!" said Helen, clasping Bernice by the shoulders. "He'll be the first one back—not counting

Bob, of course. Is he coming home or to the Veterans Hospital?"

"The way I heard it, he's coming home, but as an outpatient to the hospital. He may have to have some operations or something, but he doesn't need to be there full time."

"Oh that's a blessing!" said Helen. "It's a very nice hospital, but I'm sure he'd rather be home."

"And of course have all of us around," Bernice added.

"Well, yes of course," Helen laughed. "Who wouldn't want all of us around?"

"Where's Joanie today?" Bernice asked, pointing to a cookie and raising her eyebrows hopefully.

"Sure, have it," said Helen. "She's helping Annie this week. Since it's getting so close to Christmas, there's a lot that has to be done."

"I sure hope she'll hear from Dick pretty soon," Bernice said. "I know that's like a lead wait on her heart."

"And how," said Helen, shaking her head sadly.

"But good news first," said Bernice. "I'm going to the grocery store for a while and see what I can arrange for Henry's mother."

"Oh I'm sure she could use the help!" Helen said. "Having Henry back home safe and sound, and on the mend is a miracle. But full-time care for a while, and all of the cooking will leave her with much less time for her job at the hospital."

"That's exactly what I was thinking," Bernice mused. "Even if she can't work full hours, we can definitely help with the food. I wonder if he'll have to have any special diet."

"Protein, that's all I know. Lots of protein."

"Nice music, by the way, Helen. You got a man hidden in the closet somewhere?"

"Oh you've guessed my secret," said Helen flatly. "Now what do I tell the girls at Sodality?"

Hours later, Bernice found herself knocking on an old familiar door. The paint was chipping but it was the same color, and the hinge was still loose, dropping the door down half an inch, making it just a little challenging to open and close.

Her heart was pounding like a rabbit's, caught in a trap and worried about what was coming next. Unlike the rabbit, though, Bernice was thrilled to be seeing her old boyfriend, turned friend, and only slightly nervous. After all, it had been quite a while and time had a way of creating strangers among friends.

She knocked on the door, making sure *not* to go in at the same time. Henry's mother's call had been such a surprise. She had never expected to receive an invitation the very day he got in. But his mother had not gotten more than a few hours off of her job, and Bernice's presence was not only welcome, but necessary.

"Hey, what are you waiting for," a familiar voice called, "a marching band?"

Bernice burst out laughing, opened the door, and ran for an embrace at the bedside of her companion.

"Gee you're looking good," Henry said enthusiastically. "Even prettier than I remembered!"

"You look pretty good yourself!" Bernice said. "A little on the thin side though. Was that your rib cage?"

"Yeah, low rations and all," Henry said. "Gosh it's great to see you."

"Okay, okay," said Bernice, pulling a chair up to his bed. "This is a nice set up."

Henry's bed was neatly placed in a side room off the kitchen, within hearing distance of the outside door, the kitchen, and depending on the power in Henry's lungs, the living room on the other side of the kitchen. "Yeah," he said. "Ma's a genius. This used to be a storage room. Look how nice she made it up!"

Bernice looked around. A dark window had been cheerily draped and fringed with a pair of blue and gold curtains and the walls had been quickly covered in a light blue paint. A nice area rug covered the cement floor around Henry's bed, and a little dressing table with a mirror stood sturdily against the wall. He had a small, elegant side table by the bed, covered with a homey blue and white checked cloth. Next to it rested a pair of crutches, and a large case, open and revealing rolls of bandaging.

Cringing and looking at Henry closely, she said, "Can you walk, Henry? Those things over there look pretty ominous."

"Yes," he said quietly, reassuring her. "But I've had some surgery after the gunshot—"

"Gunshot? You got shot!" She was shocked and even a little sick to her stomach.

"Yeah," he grinned. "What'd ya think? I ate too much German food?" But he could see his dear friend was rattled, and he put his hand out, and took hers. "Listen, it's not that bad," he said, still smiling but more gently. "I know it's a shock to hear. I guess I'm hardened to a lot of stuff. But I was lucky. You know all about that." He leaned toward the side table and had a sip of water.

"That Annie's got a hell of a hero. I just hope he makes it out all right."

"What do you mean? She hasn't heard from him in a long time. Is he okay?" Henry's casual wish about Annie's fiancé put Bernice on edge. She knew her friend was trying desperately to avoid panic at having heard nothing from Sylvester for months.

Henry immediately regretted his words. "I just mean in general, you know, this is one Nasty War. What are your partners in crime up to today, by the way?"

"Joan's helping Annie at her little vesper shop over at St. Benedict's. She got that shop when her uncle went into the military."

"No kidding. That sounds like a nice way to spend the day."

"Yeah," Bernice said. "Hey let me make us some tea, okay?"

"Hey that sounds just great!" Henry said. "See if Mom's got anything in there to go with it."

"No problem," Bernice called from around the corner at the stove. "I brought some honey bread and a couple of apples."

"Terrific," Henry said. "And what's this I hear about you buying us some groceries or something? Don't be giving us food from your table."

Bernice realized that Henry's mother had given him what amounted to the short version of the story. Instead of explaining everything right then, she decided to let him rest and have his snack and they could talk about it after he had some rest. It was a lot to lay on a person. She still had trouble believing that she had money in the bank. Lots of it, even after her trusts, donations, and purchases. It would take more than a casual couple of words from around the corner to tell that story!

"Don't worry, I'm not," she answered. "Nobody loves food more than me!"

He laughed. "I think you might be second after me!" His voice was more cheerful than his thoughts were.

He traveled back to his last knowledge of Harry, Sly, Bobby and the rest of that company, headed into the mess west of what the guys all called Hitler's Holdout. It was a stubborn but deadly faction, in and around Florence. He had heard that their company was sent to support the British 8th Army at the Gothic Line and beyond. He had also heard it had been a blood bath.

Chapter Nine

"So who are you going to get for Margaret," Joan asked absently, as she swept up in the storeroom where Annie worked. "Gosh this place is dusty!"

"No kidding!" said Annie, who had wrapped a scarf around her head to keep the dust off of her hair. "I don't think I've done any cleaning all year. It's been such a funny time. Everything seems so out of whack, whatever that means."

Joan chuckled. "I know what you mean. You never know what's coming next, or what to depend on. It used to be you came here, I went into town to work, Helen did her things, we met on Friday afternoons to do gifts and stuff. Now it's all changed."

"Except making the gifts," Annie said. "We're really getting to be pros at that!"

"Especially you!"

"No, especially you!"

Joan turned, meaning to leave the storeroom but her heel was caught on something and she tripped and fell. "Ow!" she said, rubbing her knee. "This place is booby trapped. I think I tore my stocking."

"Well what did you trip on?" Annie said going to her aid.

"I don't know. It felt like a gap in the floor, I think."

"Let's see," Annie said, looking closely. "Oh, look! This must have been it. What in the world?"

"What?" Joan turned around to see Annie tracing her finger along a kind of indentation in the shape of a rectangle. "Oh criminy, Annie! That's a trap door in the floor!"

"Oh my gosh! I think you're right. Let's see. How do we open it up?"

"Well not being a trap door expert," Joan said, "I don't have anything to add."

Annie ignored her friend's tone and grabbed a candle off one of the shelves. "Let me get a match. Hold on."

"Don't worry! I'm not going any further!" Joan said, eying the development with trepidation.

"What do you think, there's ghosts or somethin'?" Annie said.

"You never know. An old church, an old dusty storeroom? There's bound to be something creepy in there."

Annie burst out laughing. She lit the candle and set it down. "Okay, move over."

"No problem!" Joan got up.

"Well don't leave!" Annie said.

"Not so brave by yourself, huh?" Joan chided.

"No, I just need a witness, you know, for when I find the buried treasure. That it was already here and I didn't plant it."

"Oh my gosh," said Joan. "I had no idea you were such a pirate."

"Pirate?" Annie stopped and turned around.

"Yeah, you've got a pirate complex."

"I don't think that's even a thing," said Annie. "But even if it is, I don't have it."

"Open the floor thingy, for heaven's sakes," said Joan.

"Okay, I've got a screwdriver and a hammer. We'll do this like Uncle Paulie used to open the milk cans when they got stuck."

She slipped the screwdriver just under the edge of the ridge and gently tapped it with the hammer. Right away the panel loosened. After several more taps in different spots, she felt she'd be able to open it. "Okay, now move the candle," she directed, "and stay with it when I take out the panel."

Joan moved closer cautiously. A little drop of liquid wax splashed onto the floor beside Annie. "Hey, watch out!" she said. "That stuff's hot."

"I'm trying," said Joan. "Open it!"

Annie lifted the panel and shoved it to the side. Joan held the candle over the opening. They both squinted wanting to see but fearing what they'd find.

"It's something flat," said Joan. "What's it made of?"

Annie tapped it with the screwdriver. "It's some kind of wood. And there's a label or something painted on it. Let me see if I can get it out of there." She tried to remove it in the same way she'd removed the panel. To their surprise, it was loose and very easy to lift.

"Help me get it into the shop," Annie said, while I scoot the panel back on top.

They set the box on top of one of the glass cases. It was an old wooden box, shellacked with fancy letters painted on the outside, but the letters were strange; some looked familiar but others looked more like symbols. They were painted in a blue that, even through the long life of the box, had sustained a beautiful brilliance.

"I wonder what it says," said Joan. "Let's look inside." She opened the clasp by pulling out a thin metal bar and then raising a small lever. As she lifted the thin layer of tissue paper to reveal the contents, both girls drew in their breath, amazed.

Finely, delicately, and sweetly beautiful were a richly painted collection of religious statuary. They had a brilliance and beauty neither girl had ever seen or even imagined before. The detail was striking, almost as if they were looking at real, albeit very small, people. The turn of head, the expression in the eyes, the shapes of the jaws and chin, mouth, eyes, and nose were startlingly realistic.

The artist had apparently created the Holy Family; Jesus, Mary, and Joseph, as well as St. Elizabeth, St. Zacharias, and St. John the Baptist.

As the girls carefully examined each piece, they became overwhelmed, occasionally wiping away a tear of awe. They found there were also animals in the collection. Three lambs, a cow, a donkey, and a small field dog lay below the Saints.

Then just as Annie lifted up the last little creature, a small envelope appeared underneath. On it was written "Father," in a fine and foreign looking penmanship.

The girls exchanged glances. "I didn't expect that," said Annie.

"Me neither," said Joan. "We gotta show Helen and Bernice!"

Not far away, Bernice was finding that caring for Henry, at least her first days' worth, was something she really enjoyed. Just as she had hoped and expected, Henry had eaten and promptly fallen asleep.

What does he dream about, she wondered. Hopefully it's a mix of things and not so much the moments surrounding his injury.

She sat quietly, thinking about where her life had been, all of the stops and starts in such recent history. Not quite a year before she had been sure that her life's mission was to enter the convent and work with the Benedictine Sisters in Philadelphia. In her innocence, she had even packed a bag and journeyed to the convent, expecting to begin her studies right then and there.

How her heart was broken by the news that even before her postulancy, she was required to discern for a year. She had thought it unfair, a waste of time, and cruel. Nevertheless, she'd complied faithfully. But then had come the death of Uncle Louie, and with it, the life altering Will in which she had been named the primary heir of a fortune. His prosperity had been amassed entirely in secret, completely unknown to Bernice or any other member of her family.

It was certainly not unwelcome. Bernice was a practical person and saw a great many needs in the world, some even as close as in her own home. But wealth would certainly separate her from the

Sisterhood, one of the vows being that of Poverty. She realized then why she had been gently led away. At least for a time.

Since that fateful, wonderful, but transformational day, she had developed a managerial ability. Not that managing things was anything new to her. Bernice had always enjoyed a natural ability to administrate, matching need to means. But playing the role of the benefactor was new and broadened her perception of the "other side."

Yet, while she enjoyed the role, it was not her calling. It was temporary, she believed. And sitting with Henry that afternoon, she knew it.

"How long you been sittin' there, Doc?" Henry asked sleepily through half opened eyes.

Bernice smiled and stood up. "You feeling okay?"

"Yes I am," Henry said. "I apologize for my rudeness, falling asleep on you and all."

Bernice laughed. "Well you should! What is the world of wounded soldiers coming to, anyway?"

"We didn't get to take that class," Henry said. "We was too rushed to get onto the field."

"How about something to drink?" Bernice asked.

"Yeah, in a minute. Take it easy. Talk to me."

Bernice sat back down. "Okay." She flicked away a tear, casually, hoping to make it look like a strand of hair.

Henry noticed. A year before, he would have said something like, "What's with the waterworks?" But he knew Bernice had gone through a huge adjustment in recent months. During his own adjustment in the multiple hospitals and aid stations he'd seen, he'd

Book 3 page 85

learned it was better to let people get to things in their own time.

"So what all did you do in Italy?" Bernice said a little too lightly.

"A lot of running," Henry said smiling.

"You had to run from the enemy?" Bernice asked, not sure what he meant.

"In a way. Our job was to watch for the drops, which means stuff they threw outta the planes, hide in the bushes, and in the dead of night, retrieve it, whatever it was, and run like mad to the connections that needed it."

Bernice's eyes were wide in astonishment. "You *what?* Oh, you're joking again, aren't you."

Henry shook his head.

"So you ran around in the middle of the night, carrying, what? Guns and stuff? Right in the middle of enemy territory?"

"Pretty much," Henry said. "Not just me, of course, and it wasn't just weapons. We mostly ran food, big crates of food and supplies. It went to people who are much braver than I am."

Bernice shook her head slowly from side to side. "I don't think *anybody's* braver than you are!" she said slowly.

Henry laughed and took her hand. "You are just the tonic I need!" he said. "Come on, let's play some gin rummy. We can talk about all that later."

Later that day and across town, at St. Benedict's Rectory, Father Bertrand was contemplating life's happiness. It had been years since Father Bertrand had shared a home with anyone, except for Kitty, of course.

Many of the younger priests were doing chaplain duty, and it had been several years before the war since there had been a second priest in residence. The senior Monsignor's presence was a warmly welcome one. Each day some unfamiliar invention or technology astonished the older gentleman. He presented questions of almost childlike proportion to Father Bertrand.

"So all of the homes are provided with heat that comes from the central?" he asked one day. "They don't use the coal?"

"I think most of the houses around here are heated with oil or electricity," Father had answered. "But we still have fireplaces. You never know when there might be an emergency."

"Yes, the emergencies," Monsignor had said, drifting for a moment. "It's important to be prepared for them."

Father Bertrand had shifted the topic just then, hoping to stave off any journeys into the dark, horrific past Monsignor possessed. The man had been in an English hospital for months, suffering from who knows what experiences. Yet, apart from occasional drifting off during conversation, the man remained strong, solid, and full of fun and good cheer. His work around the parish of the preceding months had been a great and badly needed gift to the parish.

That night, Father was making a cabbage and sausage dinner, while Monsignor took a short nap in the rocking chair by the fire. He had just set the dishes on the table when he heard a tap on the door.

"Don't just walk in!" Annie said to Bernice at the doorstep.

"Yeah!" said Joan.

"I wasn't gonna!" hissed Bernice as the door began to open.

"Oh hello girls," Father Bertrand said, stepping back. "Come on in out of the cold."

The three girls entered but huddled near the door.

"We just came to deliver something, Father," Annie said, reaching into her purse for the envelope she and Joan had discovered. "We weren't sure if you would be home until dinner time, so we dropped by now."

"I hope we're not disturbing your dinner," Joan added.

The girls could easily smell the sizzling sausages drifting in from the kitchen. It made them subconsciously lean in that direction.

"No, we haven't started yet," Father said, as he accepted the envelope from Annie. "What have we here?"

"Well, I was working in the storeroom at the church earlier—" Annie began.

Joan cleared her throat.

"We were *both* working in there," Annie corrected, "and we come across this kinda trap door."

"Trap door?" Father was intrigued.

"Yes," Joan continued. "I caught my heel on it. It was just beyond the shelves under some things. Annie pried it up with a screwdriver, and there was this box."

"Inside the box," Annie said, "is the most beautiful and detailed nativity statues you evah seen!" She couldn't keep herself from raising both hands as she said it. "Beautiful stuff! We left 'em over in the shop. Best to keep them safe, and in the box."

"Also inside the box was the letter," Joan finished. "And we didn't know who 'Father' was, but you seem like the most likely person."

"Smart thinking," Bernice said under her breath.

Annie elbowed her.

Monsignor had awakened, and seeing the 4 of them standing at the door invited them to come in.

"Thank you very much," Joan answered, "but we've got to get to Helen's house—Helen Ashenbach— for dinner. We just wanted you to have the letter."

Father had opened it and found it to be in a language he did not understand. Monsignor peered over his shoulder. After a few moments, he began to smile. He took the letter from Father to get a better look, continuing to read briefly. Then he closed his eyes, turned his face skyward, and whispered a brief prayer.

"This is a special," he said. "The letter, what you found, is so very special."

Joan and Annie were closest to him and could see his eyes glistening with tiny tears. Bernice shoved in so she wouldn't miss what the man said.

"What does it say, Alphonse?" Father Bertrand asked.

"It says the miniatures were created for and belonged to the Lithuanian Mindaugas royal family, of the Grand Duchy of Lithuania. They were created by some European monks in Italy as a special thank you."

"See? It'ly!" Annie whispered, elbowing Joan.

"It doesn't say what for," Monsignor continued. "This was over a hundred years ago. As an important favor to the royals, though, they were taken out of the country in 1877, because they feared that Russia would overcome them again, and steal them as they had stolen many other precious religious articles before. The letter is anonymous, but I think it is addressed to Father just to be certain that the articles stay in a sacred place, as they were blessed by an Archbishop."

Father and Monsignor exchanged glances. "Well that's a more proper homecoming for you," Father Bertrand said smiling.

Monsignor Kuchesky said nothing but smiled back.

"Homecoming?" Bernice asked.

"Those statues, an ancient beloved Nativity Collection, were one of the many things feared destroyed by the Nazis," Father explained. "They were considered a national treasure. I guess only a few people knew that they'd been sent here well in advance of today's demonic behaviors. And of all places, they found refuge in the very church that Monsignor would one day come to visit."

Monsignor had taken out a handkerchief and was dabbing his eyes, but merrily. "Yes, this very St. Benedict's," he said. "We must go to see them, Father."

"We would have brought them," Annie began, "but it didn't seem like—"

"Not at all," Monsignor objected. "No. You have done the perfectly right thing! You left them in safety, as they should be."

"Yes, indeed," said Father Bertrand. "Are they in the shop?"

After Annie had explained exactly where they were, the girls said goodbye and left, holding hands and fairly skipping merrily down the sidewalk.

Chapter Ten

The wind tousled Laureen's hair as she struggled against it, plodding down the sidewalk to Annie and Joan's house. She felt the tiny pellets of ice striking her nose, telltale signs that a South Jersey ice storm was on the way.

I should have tied this scarf a little tighter, she thought, pulling the edges of it closer around her face. But the wind instantly returned it to its original place, mixing in a few extra bits of ice as well. She shivered and picked up her pace.

"Here she comes," said Annie, looking out the window. "She'll be ready for that cup of coffee, Joan. The sleet is already coming down!" She hurried over to open the door.

Laureen pounded her feet to kick off the ice and quickly stepped inside. "Thanks," she said smiling as Annie took her coat. "It's nasty out there!"

"We should have planned this for another day," Joan said. "Hi Laureen! Good to see you!"

Laureen turned, and seeing her dear friend reaching out for a hug, innocent of the life shattering knowledge that she possessed, burst into tears.

Annie and Joan stood for a second or two, completely thrown, mouths open, staring.

"What did I *say?*" Joan whispered to Annie.

Annie shook her head and shrugged her shoulders. Gently she took Laureen by the elbow and encouraged her to take a seat. Joan fetched a handkerchief from the buffet.

"Oh I'm so sorry," Laureen puffed, shaking her head and exhaling. "That's been welling up inside for a couple of days."

Still confused but relieved, Joan said, "So it wasn't anything I said?"

"No!" Laureen half laughed. "It's, it's just that I saw you and I just thought, well, I have to start at the beginning. This whole situation with Bob has really shaken me," she said. "You know? I have always been pretty clear on what to do, what to expect, basically everything."

"You have always given me great advice," Joan said, nodding. "You always know what to do."

Laureen smiled and went on. "But with Bob feeling the way he is, not wanting me to come see him, I guess it has had me rattled. I haven't felt this way since I tripped and fell going to First Holy Communion when I was eight years old."

Laureen laughed nervously, and the others joined her, not sure how to react. "But anyway, I decided to go and see Bob, no matter what Helen said, and my Mom, and probably you two if I had bothered to ask your opinion," she said.

"You saw Bob?" Joan said.

"No."

"Oh." Joan looked at Annie.

"No. I got as far as just outside his door. But I stopped."

Annie and Joan were nodding in sympathy, but still thoroughly confused.

"They had these chairs and I spilled everything out of my purse," Laureen said, starting to cry again.

"Oh, that's too bad," Annie said, trying to comfort her.

"No, it was okay," Laureen said. "I got it all back in my purse. I just, oh." She sighed. "Okay let me just say it, Joan, and get it over with."

"Me? Well, now you're definitely scaring me."

"I'm so sorry. I heard Bob tell Father Bertrand that his good friend Dick, so it had to be your fiancé, had been shot."

"Shot?" was all Joan said.

"It wasn't a bad wound to begin with, but that it had become infected, and apparently throughout his body. And he was sick, burning up with fever." Laureen collapsed into sobs. "And he was supposed to come here, but he never arrived."

Joan's breath suddenly came hard, almost as if she were being strangled. She tried to shake it off. "Never arrived. Well how long has it been since he was supposed to have arrived?"

"Bob got here weeks ago," Laureen sobbed. "I don't know. That was all I heard."

"Did Bob say Dick was," Joan tried to continue but she could not form the word.

Annie put an arm around Joan and patted Laureen's hand. "Joanie," she said, "that don't mean nothin'. You know how these big organizations are. Everybody's always gettin' lost. They prob'ly sent 'im to Antarctica or somethin' by mistake. Don't take it to heart. You know how them people are."

Laureen nodded. "I thought of that. It could be that, Joan. Just because Bob doesn't know where he is, it doesn't mean something's happened to him."

Joan was separating momentarily. Was he sick? Was Dick 'burning up with fever'? How could that be? He never sounded like that in his letters. Had he even written the letters? Had he actually died and someone else was pretending to write his letters?

It was too horrible to fathom. And she couldn't slow down the thoughts. They were coming at her like snowballs, fast and hard, bursting right onto her chest, taking away her breath. But Dick had just written. No, hold on. That was weeks ago, she thought. When *was* that? Had she even bothered to read the date? "When was he, I mean when did he last write?" she asked Laureen. Then realizing that was the wrong person, she looked at Annie and repeated herself.

"I can't remember, I guess it was September, October maybe?" Annie said, trying to remember. "So a couple of months or less, I guess."

"Maybe it's a different friend named Dick," Joan said to Laureen, her eyes appealing it to be true.

Laureen just looked back at her, sorry and sad at once and wanting so to have the same natural optimism.

"We don't actually *know*," Joan said, looking at Annie.

"No, we don't know," she said.

The ice pounded against the window, reminding the girls that they were safe, dry, and warm inside. But for once, Joan felt only the chill in that sign of winter. The coziness had gone out of it.

Way across the country, on that very same day, in a veterans' hospital in Oklahoma, Dick Thimble lay sleeping on one of the specially equipped beds reserved for the most severely infirmed. His body was ravaged by the weeks of inactivity and low caloric intake. To add insult to injury, during his nightmare and subsequent fall to the hard floor, he had broken his arm. It lay by his side, but heavily clad in plaster, at an awkward angle.

Dick was not fully aware of that fact, but as what would come as a great surprise to his medical team, he was aware of where he was.

Silently, he lay thinking, studying the ceiling, the grooves in it and cobwebs at the corners. A nearby light stood alert, at attention, Dick thought, amusing himself. It may be at attention, but its bulb's burnt out. That made him smile, thinking of conversations he and Bob had had at the expense of some of their buddies at basic training.

Bob, what a good old guy, he thought. He journeyed right alongside me, kept me going, boy. I wonder. . . His mind dimmed a little, struggling to remember the recent past. Had Bob been hit? Surely he was still alive.

The light in the room is soft, so it must be daytime, he thought. Day time. I am in a hospital, that much I know. I think I'm in London. Or was that before? No, the Aid Station was before. Yes, this must be London. The Sisters in blue habits.

He took a breath and found that it was a bit of a struggle. How long has it been since I had a good old breakfast, he wondered. Coffee. Oh I could sure use a cup of coffee. But this arm, here. What's going on there? Oh, yes, that fall that time. When was that?

As he turned his head slightly to examine his arm, the nurse in the ward was instantly on alert. In seconds, she was by his side.

"Sgt. Thimble? Sgt. Thimble, I'm here. Can you hear me?"

Dick focused his eyes on the figure in motion. Oh my, he thought. She's wearing black. That can't be good. Then he recognized the habit. A Sister of Divine Providence. But that was Yankee, that was American. Where was he?

"Can you hear me, Sgt. Thimble?"

"Oh, yes, I'm sorry," he said, his voice hardly a whisper. It came out so faintly that it startled him. It did not startle Sister Veronica Ann.

She smiled broadly, touched his shoulder and said, "That's music to my ears! I'm going to get the doctor." She moved away quickly, then turned back momentarily and said with a twinkle, "Don't get up."

Dick chuckled and instantly went back to sleep, the smile fixed on his lips.

Chapter Eleven

"It's been a while since we had any of these kinds of meetings," Harry said. "It may seem unnecessary at this point, but the fact is, there are new threats that we all need to be aware of."

Sylvester and Bobby hunched forward against the cold. Several others had joined Harry's company in getting ready for the impending action. The Allies had a goal of once and for all stabilizing Allied control of the Gothic Line. That line was essentially the division between Axis and Allied territories. It had been heavily fortified for several years with minimal penetration by the Allies. But there had been progress that fall, and the Allies largely regarded it as broken. But not everyone was able to accept the Nazi defeat. The German Commander simply would not let it go.

"We'll be behind the line, as usual, close by Florence," Harry was saying. "But that doesn't mean we have clear sailing. Kesselring has no intention of giving up the fight. And it has been discovered that the area south and north of the Gothic is infiltrated with tenacious German soldiers. It is *essential* that we stay alert to any indications of snipers, mines, etc."

Bobby shook his head. "Them mines," he said. "They get me so damn edgy."

Sly nodded. How could a soldier spot something partially concealed, underground? There had been more than one occasion where men had been there one minute and gone the next.

"That's not all," Harry went on. "You've got your Nazi sympathizers. This country is divided, men. This whole time it's been back and forth, and don't kid yourself thinking just because the ruling government is on our side that all the civilians are. There are those in league with Hitler. Many of them are not content to watch us push up through this country. So you're not on the lookout for Germans only. You're going to have to be aware of any enemy action or suspicious bit of behavior anywhere."

Great, Sly thought. I can just see explaining my missing leg to Annie. Well, you see dear, there were those who didn't agree with us. It made his stomach turn.

Bobby gave him a look. It was a bitter pill. The Allies had made progress, they'd moved well into France since the famous landings on the coast. And Rome had been liberated there in Italy. But freeing the capital apparently meant nothing, especially in a divided country.

"We are fortunate to have with us members of the elite French le corps Expéditionnaire Français, which is a French-led group who fought in North Africa. Their expertise is in mountain areas, and they can be of great service to our unit. Most of them will be with the forward companies, of course, but we have Robert and Claude with us."

The men acknowledged each other as Harry finished up his instructions by listing break out groups and individual duties.

"It's cooling down, but there's no snow in the forecast. If we can stay with the Command before the heavy rains set in, we might be able to achieve our objective. All right. Get your rations and some sleep. Tomorrow's going to be a long day."

Harry's words turned out to be prophetic. The day started with an unexpected rainstorm. The rain and wind added weight and struggle to the company, who were far enough behind the frontline to miss out on any of the more substantial protection from the weather. Front liners carried small packs or kits to create screen houses, like tents but with wooden structures. The Communications company had only tents, and many of them were in serious need of patching and repair.

As the rain continued, puddles developed along the pathways. Robert urged the men to move into the wooded area and take refuge before they hit the less protected hills ahead.

"I'm inclined to agree," Harry said. "We'll set up where Robert and Claude feel is most appropriate."

They selected a small clearing within a level area surrounded by cedar and other evergreens. Pitching tents in the rain was an activity Sly and Bobby had gotten quite good at. Once theirs was set, they helped the less experienced fellows, and then went to get water from a nearby pond.

"There might be fish in there, too," Bobby said. "Wish I had my stuff."

"Really? You go fishing? A city boy like you?"

"Oh yeah! My uncle takes me down the shore there, and we get striper, flounder, sometimes we even get crabs in the back bays."

"Yeah, crabbing's fun, ain't it?" said one of the other men. "You just set up the trap and have a smoke, and wait for 'em to climb in."

Bobby chuckled. "Yeah, but in my case, I'd probably go through a pack of Luckys." He coughed. "I gotta give these damn things up."

There was no fish that night though. Returning with a large canvas type skin of water, the men set it down on some stones and let the company cook know about it.

"Hey, thanks guys," he said. "Saved me a trip and a lot of aggravation."

"I would not drink that," Claude said, looking warily at the water. "We don't know about these puddles."

Sly and Bobby exchanged glances. "It didn't come from no puddle," Bobby said indignantly. "We got it out the lake."

"The Lake?" Claude repeated. He had been searching for the word "pond" but used "puddle" instead. He was unfamiliar with "lake."

"Okay, it wasn't a huge lake, but it wasn't no puddle," Bobbie said. "Listen, that's gotta be good water. It's fresh rain, ain't it?"

Claude shook his head, confused.

Sly misunderstood the gesture. "I don't know how you would know. You're not from around here, are you?" he demanded.

"I am not," Claude said.

"What's the trouble?" Harry asked.

"He thinks we got this water from a puddle," said Bobby. "It ain't from no puddle, it's fresh rainwater from the lake."

"We could be having a language barrier," Harry said. He motioned to Claude. "It's okay. The water is fresh."

Claude shrugged and took a seat on a rock by the mess tent, shielded by an overhanging cedar.

"Them French guys," Bobby said.

"We don't need any of that, Sgt. Pitro," Harry said harshly. He gave Bobby a stern look and turned to talk with the cook.

"You gotta watch that stuff, city boy," Sly teased. "He's right. There's no room for dissention. We're all on the same side."

"Yeah, yeah, yeah," Bobby said.

"We'd better see that the water's boiled," Sly said. "I don't want dysentery, that's for sure."

"Yo, it's fresh from the sky!" Bobby insisted. "How's it gonna be contaminated?"

As the rain continued to fall, the little pond was rapidly filling, its banks overflowing. Miniature ripples made their way to the water's edge, accompanied by tiny fish. At the one end of the pond, a tree trunk lay, its rich mossy bark beginning to float on the rising water. The profile of the fallen tree was interrupted by the little hills and valleys created when shells of a machine gun had once spattered the area. At the other end of the pond, now fully submerged, lay the body into which the bullets had taken up residence.

As the cook boiled gallons of water, Sly stood close, hoping to dry off a little and warm himself.

"You got it all under control, or can I lend a hand?"

"Thanks, Sir," the man said. "I gotta get these rations out, but other than the coffee, we don't have much else going."

"It's better than nothing!" Sly said. "Let me have some. I'll hand 'em out."

Before long, the coffee was finished perking and the small company was refreshed from their evening meal of spam, crackers, and candy bars.

"I miss my Em's cookin'," said one of the men. "That's the first thing I'm going to have when I get home."

"Yeah, this stuff stinks," said another man. "But it beats going hungry."

Robert and Claude exchanged glances. "You don't know what it is to go hungry," said Claude. "In my country they are starving. I don't mean they are hungry; they are starving."

The Americans were startled.

"He is not joking," said Robert. "There are people who have eaten their family animals, their, what is the word, their pet."

Bobby looked at Sly. "I think I'm going to be sick."

Sly chuckled. "Ain't nobody gonna eat your cat," he whispered.

"No, seriously, I think I'm going to be sick," Bobby said. And he quickly got behind a tree and reversed peristalsis.

When he'd come back to the tent, Sly said, "Seriously? That story made you so sick you threw up?"

"No. I've been feeling kind of weird ever since. . ."

"Ever since when?" Sly asked.

"Yes, ever since when?" Claude demanded.

Bobby looked sheepishly at him. "I was so thirsty. I didn't want the coffee. I wanted a cup of water. I. . ." Bobby's face was growing paler. He exited the tent again, with great urgency, but less energy.

"What's happening?" Sly asked Claude. "Is that water poison?"

"I don't know," Claude answered. "But in these woods, there was a lot of fighting. The water could be contaminated. Remember, there could be old refuse in that pond, dead animals, or dead. . ." He stopped, unwilling to speak disparagingly of the fallen brothers.

That evening, the rain continued, and Bobby stayed in his tent, missing out on the shared stories between the French, Italian, and American soldiers. The rain was a salve during the war. Very few, if any, commanders would launch assaults in the rain. There were too many unknowns. The threat of casualties before even engaging with the enemy was too great. So the rain, for both sides, signified a temporary relief from the war, often accompanied by stories, laughter, and alcohol.

Chapter Twelve

It was an icy 12 degrees in Abbottsville that morning. Joan rose earlier than usual in order to make morning Mass. The mirror told the tale of her hours of tears from the night before and she knew she would need extra time with a moist washcloth before she put on her face. How could Dick have gone missing? How could the Army just lose him? Or *had* they actually lost them? Bob was pretty sick himself. Maybe he was confused, or just didn't actually have the full picture. Or maybe Dick had actually recovered, gotten all well and been sent out again. But that thought didn't do much to cheer her either.

She took a deep breath, feeling weighted down by fatigue and distress. As she brushed her teeth, she prayed fervently for her fiancé, as she and the girls had done the day before. She prayed for herself. She felt selfish, but she knew she needed help and there was only one place to seek it. Dick's pain was her pain; they were indivisible. *Please let him be all right!*

"You okay?" Annie said from the hall, startling her. "I'm up and ready. I'm going with you."

"Oh that's great, thanks, Annie." She gave her a hug. "Yes, I'm okay. I thought about it most of the night. We don't know anything, and if we don't know anything, there's nothing to be upset about."

"That's the way I force myself to look at it," Annie said, leaning against the sink. "Do you know how long it's been since I have had any word at all about Sylvester?"

"I know," Joan said. "It's all of us. I was just lucky for a little while. But Annie, Helen hasn't heard a word from Harry in a long time, either. Probably the longest of all of us."

"I know. But remember, she hasn't heard a word *about* him either, and that's what we keep hoping for. Just stay safe, stay out of danger."

"Yes, stay out of the dangerous part of the War." Joan stifled a smile.

Annie laughed out loud. "That's pretty much it," she said. "Listen, it's a special day. Let's go to the diner after church."

"I would love that. And if this wild feeling is out of my stomach by then, I'll even eat something."

"It will be."

As the two of them bundled up, preparing for the multi-block walk through the icy wind, a knock came on the door.

"I knew you two would be up," Bernice said opening the door and peering around it.

"Me, too," said Helen. "I hope you're all bundled up. It's not supposed to get above 20 today." She smiled warmly at Joan. "In case you're wondering, Annie filled us in."

Joan smiled back as bravely as she could, her lips quivering. "No, this is wonderful," she said, stepping outside. "Come on, let's storm the heavens together."

St. Benedict's Church was dimly lit with a combination of electric light and eternally burning rows of candles positioned just below the statue of the Blessed Mother. Incense was perpetually burning, the sweet scent bringing peace to many troubled hearts.

The little church had been standing a long time. Father Bertrand's tenure had experienced ebb and flow of daily Mass attendees. However, over the most recent years, there had been a consistently growing number present. Many came for comfort, others to pray for special intentions, and still others praying for peaceful repose of souls they had known.

The morning Mass was always short so as to allow folks to attend on their way to work. The men and women with jobs huddled together at the bus stop on the corner. Joan felt a wishful pang as she passed by. It had been tough rising so early every morning to go to work the previous year, but it would certainly take her mind away from sad things if she had a job.

Annie raced ahead to open the door to the diner. Inside, it was bright and welcoming. The familiar scent of waffles and syrup hung in the toasty warmth as they took their seats in a booth at the window.

The two waitresses operated in high gear, crisscrossing, serving up full plates of eggs and toast, coffee and milk, their trays whipping in and out of booths at almost alarming speed.

"This is just what the doctor ordered!" said Helen, taking out her reading glasses.

"What?" said Joan, peering at the menu. "The bacon and eggs?"

Bernice giggled and elbowed Annie.

"Yes," said Annie. "Doctors frequently order high protein meals."

"What?" said Joan.

Helen shook her head, smiling. "Leave her alone."

"What?" Joan repeated.

"It's an expression," said Bernice. "You know, like the cat's meow, or the bee's knees? Just what the doctor ordered."

"Oh, no kidding. I never heard that before," Joan said, returning to her menu.

Bernice went on. "But personally I think the doctor would order the fruit plate."

"Large or small?" The waitress was right at her elbow.

Helen stifled a laugh.

"Oh! No, I wasn't ordering," Bernice said hastily.

"Didn't you just say you wanted the fruit platter?" the waitress demanded.

"I did, but I was—"

"All right, I'll give you girls a minute to make up your minds." And she was off in a flash.

Annie and Joan giggled.

"She's a stealthy little thing, isn't she?" Helen said.

Just then, before Bernice could respond, an ominously familiar redhead walked by, arm-in-arm with another person Joan recognized. The redhead was Gloria Marini, Joan's seemingly eternal competitor for the love and affection of the handsome Dick Thimble. It had not seemed to matter to Gloria that Dick was engaged. She had tried several dirty tricks in the past to try to steal him away from Joan, starting with spilling a drink on Joan's only dress when she'd just met him.

But on that day at the diner, it looked as if Miss Marini had finally found herself her own gentleman. She paused after she passed their booth to turn and give Joan a superior look. She clutched the arm of Joan's former manager, an eligible fellow indeed with a nice income. Seeing that Joan had recognized her companion, she tossed her perfectly styled head of red curls and strutted on to another booth beyond them.

Joan let out a sigh.

Annie grimaced and shook her head.

"Remember what mother says," Helen said in a cheerful voice. "If you can't think of something nice to say, then don't say anything at all."

"I think this is going to be one quiet table," said Bernice. "Except me. I got stuff to say. I want to tell you all about how well Henry's doing. That is after I order a nice big breakfast of scrapple and fried eggs."

"Do you want juice with that?" the waitress asked.

Further into the diner, the ever-alert Gloria watched for envy or at least a little discomfort at the girls' table. Seeing none, she decided it might be a good time to go to the powder room.

"Excuse me, Dear," she said sweetly to her date. "I've got to go powder my nose. Be right back!"

She sacheted her way toward Joan's table just as the waitress was setting a cup of coffee next to Joan. This is going to be fun, she thought. She and her forty-nine-dollar ankle strapped blue leather heels with gold ornaments pranced over to the booth.

"Hello, Joan and friends," she said a little too sweetly. "I see the early morning crowd is here." She leaned forward quickly, her pocketbook hitting the coffee cup, intentionally knocking it over. Her intended victim leaned back and dodged it successfully. But Joan needn't have bothered. The saucers were high and round. As the cup tipped over, the hot liquid shot up, deflected itself from the edge of the saucer, and back over the opposite side, covering Gloria's skirt, stockings, and dripping liberally onto her blue leather heels, right down to the gold ornament.

"Oh!" she wailed. "Oh my beautiful shoes! You, you clumsy. . . clumsy ox!" she finished, and turned, heading hurriedly to the ladies room.

It had all happened so rapidly that only Joan was sure what had gone on.

"How did she get coffee on her clown shoes?" Annie asked.

Bernice started to laugh and tried desperately to hold it in.

"She knocked over my coffee!" Joan said. "I think she did it on purpose, too!"

"My stars!" said Helen.

The show had not gone unnoticed. The waitress, who seemingly never paused long enough to catch her breath, stood stock still with an expression of incredulity on her face. "Why'd she do that?" she asked, speaking to no one. But her break had gone on too long already and off she went, tossing a quick, "I'll get you another," over her shoulder.

"Did she get you, Joan honey?" Helen asked, straining across the booth to see if there was any coffee on Joan's dress.

"Not a drop," said Joan. "I think we should tell her thank you."

"For *not* spilling coffee on you that she clearly intended to spill on you?" Annie said.

"No. Because if we needed a good distraction from our misery, she did a great job!"

The girls forced themselves to act normally when a rinsed and considerably less glamorous Gloria passed by to return to her seat, apparently failing to notice them.

"So I have a story to tell you guys," Bernice said. "Henry told me how he got hurt."

"Do we want to hear this?" Annie said.

"Listen, I'm not going to tell gory details. Actually, I don't know any gory details. I just wanted to tell you something, you and Helen especially."

"Should I excuse myself?" Joan asked facetiously.

"Yes," said Bernice.

"Well I'm not going to."

"Okay. Henry was a sprinter."

"A what?"

"Sprinter. They're a special service that retrieves important stuff that they throw from planes in the dead of night," Bernice explained. "His job, along with his team's, was to go to appointed areas, and wait completely concealed."

"Did he wear that makeup they wear in the movies?"

"Huh? Wait a minute, what?"

"You know, they put that like black shoe polish or something on their skin to keep it from reflecting in the moonlight."

"Oh. Gosh I don't know. Geeze, Annie, you know more about this than I do."

"No, no, I'm sorry, go ahead, Bernice."

"Yeah, okay. So one night, they get some help from some other guys, and on that particular night, out of nowhere these rifles start blasting. One of the guys gets stuck on the field under fire, and Henry removes the threat, I think is how he said it. But just as he's moving back off the field and toward the brush, he's hit. And hit really bad."

"Oh my gosh, Henry?" Helen asked.

"Yeah, Henry," Bernice went on. "So the guy he was protecting turns around and finishes off the guy that shot Henry. Then they carry him, I mean *carry* him, bleeding like mad, all the way back to camp, like over two miles away. These guys took him into what he called 'the caves.' He said he can't say anymore about it, but it was a safe area. There was a good medic there. Let me tell you, Annie, if them guys had left him and gone back for a medic, he'd be gone today."

"Yeah? That's heroic."

"You're not kidding, because they didn't know if there were more Nazis or Nazi sympathizers around. They just took their chances and carried him."

"How come you're telling Annie?" Joan said. "I care about Henry, too."

Helen smiled. "I bet I know why."

"You'd be right," said Bernice. She paused and gave Annie a rare sincere smile. "Them guys was Bobby Pitro and his buddy Sylvester Bapini."

Annie gasped. "No!"

"Yeah!"

"Oh!" She grasped Helen's hand. "Oh my gosh. I don't know what to say." She fought back a tear.

"He's a hero, Annie," Joan said, beaming. "He's a genuine hero."

"But he wasn't hurt?" Annie asked suddenly.

"No, no, Henry saved him. Then he saved Henry, he and Bobby."

Annie leaned back against the booth and let out a sigh. It was as if a marching band had just crossed her chest.

Helen put an arm around her. "That was a wonderful story," she said. "This has started out to be a really nice day!"

"Oh but it ain't over yet," said Bernice. "So he's in the caves, the medic is helping, right. But Henry was hit really bad, and the medic knows it. He's stopped the bleeding but it's a deep body wound and there's going to be infection. It's too dangerous to get him on a transport out, even by water. His Command was a mobile one that met this cargo as it got dropped off in a lot of places. They couldn't stick around and get him out, because the Resistance depended on them getting the things they needed, guns and food and stuff. So the Commander of the Comm Division and a couple really brave guys traveled through the cave network, at incredible risk, to get him to a very small, very secret launch where a small boat would get him to a friendly harbor. And they made it!"

She turned and looked at Helen. "And guess who the Communications boss was?"

"Oh Holy Mother of God," Helen said, her voice cracking. She dabbed at her eyes with a lacy blue handkerchief. "The crazy fool," she said smiling through tears.

"Captain Harry Ashenbach," Bernice finished. "I bet you guys liked that story."

"You can say that again," said Annie. "I'm happy to hear that they're all together. At least that they were when all of this happened this summer. I wonder where they are now."

Joan squeezed her hand and smiled. "Probably out saving somebody else."

In fact, Bobby and Sylvester were in the midst of a near monsoon period in Italy. The day following Bobby's ill-fated experiment with unsanitized water, the rain had begun to advance beyond the shores of the little pond, carrying water plants and silt along with it. Word had come from the front that their company was to stay put, so the soldiers whose tents were threatened by the water were rapidly repositioning them onto higher ground.

It was around 2 o'clock that afternoon, when Claude and Sylvester were doing a quick surveillance of the pond that the washed-up body was discovered.

Claude, the first to discover it, quickly bowed and made the sign of the cross.

"What is it?" asked Sly.

Claude motioned with his head. "Left behind," was all he said.

Sly's eyes grew wide. Marone! The body was still in its uniform, not one hundred percent preserved, which was evident from the hollowness of the uniform where an arm should have been. Clearly, he had been dead for a long time. Sylvester was stunned. "Surely they would have retrieved any of the fallen," he said.

"Not necessarily. Especially if they were under heavy fire, or maybe even a lone soldier—we are not the first to cover this territory."

"From the looks of his uniform," Sylvester said, "I would say he's one of yours."

"Yes," said Claude. "It looks to me as if this poor devil was a front-line soldier with one of the earlier regiments, of course."

"Well, we should have a burial," said Sylvester. "Or at least a memorial service here. Perhaps you want to return him to France?"

"Yes, of course," said Claude. "It's very kind of you to concern yourself about his welfare. In France, we are not informed about the American generosity, at least not officially. I have heard of it from other soldiers though. I would like to say that I appreciate it very much. Dedication to one's own is admirable, but dedication to all is ideal. If we had more of that, we would not have this war to begin with."

"That's for sure," Sly said. "It goes both ways, Claude. Thank you."

"Yes, and right now, this soldier's memorial is not what concerns me. There is something that is much more urgent."

"What do you mean?" Sly asked.

"I mean that your friend," said Claude seriously, "the sick one called Bobby. He's in extreme danger."

Chapter Thirteen

"No doctor? What about further down, into the Allied camps? Surely—"

"No," Harry said with finality. "They've got more duty up north. The push over the line up there is intense, Sly. But we are going to have to get him out of here, and soon, before pneumonia sets in."

As Claude had predicted, Bobby had gone from reacting to dirty water to a nearly comatose state. His blood pressure was falling, and Sly feared that an old wound he'd received during the bombing of Bari the year before was causing the problem.

"You know, Cap, with the rain, I was thinking there's not going to be any action. Isn't there somewhere we can take him so he's not in this sop of an ice-cold mess 24 hours a day?"

Harry had to agree. Even inside his tent it was dripping wet. The unremitting downpour had reduced the tents to little more than shelter from actively falling rain. Inside, they were soaking wet. Touching the sides of the tent meant leakage. Touching the sides was virtually unavoidable. Bobby's head was supported by the only dry bedding that remained. Even that would not be so for long. Only impermeable canvas would help and there was none to be had.

Harry nodded. Watching Bobby continue to fail, languishing without any hope of medical aid or even comfort was twisting him inside. The two young men had been his comrades through perilous and painful times. Given the situation, in which Bobby would not be able to serve, and probably, as Sly had said, there would be no action, it seemed likely that the company of 12 would be staying put for some days to come. That could only worsen Bobby's health.

Sly knew that Harry had to be careful about favoritism. All the men in the company were valuable, contributing members of the Communications Division, down to the entry level interpreter Bobby and he had mentored. But what good was Bobby in his condition? And how long did he have before time ran out for him? He needed dry clothing and warmth to have a fighting chance.

The company clerk was speaking with Harry. Harry nodded and the man left the tent. His tone softened. In a fatherly manner, he said, "Listen, I'm hesitant to tell you this because of the potential danger involved, but I know you, and I have to make the offer. There's a sympathetic farmer north and east of here, about four miles on foot. The man has offered refuge to several members of the underground and has even hidden one man for over a month during a time when this place was crawling with Nazis. Strictly speaking, it's neither Allied nor enemy territory right now. And he's not a doctor. But his wife is a nurse. Most importantly, he could offer dry shelter."

"Yes," said Sly. "I'll take Bobby and—"

"Hold on," Harry held up his hand. "It will have to be covert, under night cover, and Sly, only you. I can't spare another man. This could lift any minute, and they'll need us out doing our thing."

"I'll go," said Sly.

Harry offered his hand. "I knew you would," he said smiling sadly as they shook.

"We'll join up with the Company just as soon as Bobby is back on his feet!"

As Sly hurried off to get packed, Harry's smile faded. He hated keeping secrets from the kid whom he thought of as a son. But adding to the mix with more sensitive issues would help no one. And Sly's success depended on his determination to get the mission accomplished. The last thing he needed was Harry's news plaguing his mind.

Harry returned to his desk and reopened the envelope he had received the day before. Orders. By the time Sly and Bobby rejoined the company, *if* they rejoined the company, Harry would be stateside, back home, out of rotation. Permanently.

Much later that night, with rain falling, much of it in the form of ice, Sylvester pulled his buddy through the dark unknown Marconi Wood in a makeshift wagon. The wheels, well oiled, silently turned with each step. Despite the cover of both dark and frozen rain, danger surrounded them like a menacing cloud. Sly's experience told him to focus on the mission. He knew he was alone, but he had a valuable charge to protect. His mission was to deliver Bobby securely through the perilous journey to safety.

He thought of Henry, the kid back home who had covered for him earlier that year. They'd journeyed through similar circumstances, but with Bobby as a protector, not a protectee.

All because of dirty water, he thought, shaking his head. All because of water contaminated by the decaying matter that had been another fighting soldier. All because of, well, because of war. He shook it off.

How can I be philosophizing, he thought. There could be a machine gun nest stuck between those three fat trees. He watched the trees, his weapon hand taut. He passed the trees, which stood innocently staring back. All right, nobody's in there. They coulda been though. They could be up behind that bunch of brush or whatever it is. But he passed by and again, there were no threatening soldiers.

Hours passed, and Sly worried that dawn would arrive before he reached the farm. Where in the world is this farm, he thought. He checked his direction the best he could on his compass, holding it close to his eyes and noting the flicker of reflection. Maybe he'd passed it. The farmhouse would have been beyond the wood, and here he was, still in the wood.

He sat for a moment, feeling the muscles in his legs stiffen as soon as they were given the chance. He massaged them and checked on Bobby for the eighth time that trip. Bobby had been unconscious most of the way, but this time, Sly asked, "You awake? How you like this little walk we're taking? We're going to the diner." He had not expected a response.

But under the blankets, he heard a muffled, "Sangwich."

He smiled. "Okay, I'll see what I can do," he said, energized from the small improvement.

Just then a crack of thunder hit somewhere so powerfully it made Sylvester jump. Subsequent short flashes of light helped him realize that he had overshot

his objective. He turned due east and struggled
through the heavy brush for another hour until at last
he arrived at a clearing. There, only a small way ahead
lay the farmhouse. He settled Bobby's wagon in a
shrubbery, making sure he was covered and obscured.

It was just before dawn. His heart was racing with
anticipation of getting Bobby safely inside, but he had
to make sure there were no snipers. If they were
anywhere, it would be here, he told himself. They'd be
at the edge of the wood, waiting for him or some other
soldier struggling to survive.

The way ahead was clear, but there was a clump of
trees just before the farmhouse. Someone could be in
there, or someone could be over there, he thought,
looking at a stack of firewood. What a perfect place for
a sniper to hide.

He made ready his rifle and shielded the works
from the rapidly increasing rain. Suddenly something
moved to his right. It could have been a rabbit, he
thought, a predawn hunt for vegetation. But then again
came a sound, the crack of a branch too heavy for a 3-
or 4-pound rabbit.

In half a second, Sly fell prone, his rifle ready,
instantly his eyes fixed on that section of wood. For a
moment, it was still. Just as he started to relax, came
another crack. He rose on one knee, leaning forward,
rifle in position.

Almost as if flipping a switch, as soon as he put up
his knee, a shot rang out but from the opposite side! Sly
turned to his left just in time to see a man running
away, carrying a pistol. He wore no uniform that Sly
could recognize in the grey light. He seemed to
disappear beyond the clump of trees.

"Why did he run away?" Sly said softly. Then, as an afterthought, he checked for injuries. To his horror his leg was bleeding badly. He hadn't felt a thing!

Immediately he thought of Bobby, some twenty yards back. *How safe was he with that man on the loose? Were there others? And why didn't I shoot the bastard,* he wondered. But Sly hadn't had a second to fire, and probably would not have hit him anyway. The sudden ugly turn in events was maddening and extremely frustrating.

Replaying things in his mind, Sly determined that the gunman must have been throwing stones in order to smoke him out. *And I fell for it. Like a rookie! And here I am, bleeding, supposed to be getting Bobby out of danger.*

He moved toward Bobby, half crawling, half walking to get under some cover of the brush. The bullet wound was starting to speak to him. How big a bullet, he wondered, trying to separate himself from the situation. *Looked like a 45. Could be. They make a nice hole. The guy must have had just the one bullet.* That thought made him chuckle.

Pull, stumble, pull, stumble, foot by foot, back into the safety of the wood. He reached Bobby, who still under the layers of canvas, was sleeping. Sly said a prayer of thanks that the gunman had not caught sight of Bobby.

He pulled some bandaging from his gunnysack and tried to do something with his wound, but the blood was flowing freely. Finally, with his last ounces of strength, he tied a sock around his leg to put pressure against the wound. He started to dream while he was still awake.

He climbed into the wagon, covered Bobby's body with his own, said another prayer and passed out.

Chapter Fourteen

"Are you still just lying around?" Bernice teased as she entered the little room behind the kitchen at Henry's house. "Seems like you were there the last time I came here."

Henry broke into a broad smile. "Don't be fooled. I ran and got in here when I heard you coming. I'm hoping for some more white glove service. You brought me some goodies, didn't you?"

"Well, I haven't gotten any reports on your behavior yet," Bernice said. "So you'll have to wait until I find out about that before you get any rewards."

"Oh, the report clipboard is over there," Henry said, pointing at the little end table. "Bring it over and I can read it to you."

At first Bernice looked for a clipboard. But quickly she caught on and grasped the make-believe report. "Here it is," she said reaching. "I don't see any gold stars." Then quickly she drew in her breath, embarrassed.

Henry's eyes met hers. He shook his head. "Hey, don't worry about it," he said soothingly.

In 1944, Gold Stars on the windows and walls meant only one thing; that there had once been a son or husband or father living there who was no longer. The battles had gone on for so long by then that that proud but heartbreaking sight was no longer rare.

Bernice nodded, but a tear fell from her eye, which she tried to disguise by turning.

Henry said nothing but patted her elbow.

She looked back at him and sniffed, shaking her head. "How do you manage it?" she asked, her voice cracking.

"Manage what, my attitude you mean?"

"Yes, your attitude, your demeanor, just everything. You had probably one of the most serious injuries, the closest brushes with death I know of. You lost a friend. But yet I don't see a hint of that bitterness."

"After all the goodies you've brought, you're expecting bitterness?" Henry teased, rising on an elbow.

"I'm very serious," Bernice said. She sighed. "A friend of mine, a new friend, is engaged to a man who was wounded in the leg. It's serious, and he doesn't know whether or not he's going to keep that leg. But there's hope, and he's here in the United States. He's here in New Jersey. But because of, of, I don't know, the injury or *something*, he won't, and I mean he *refuses* to see his fiancé. The poor girl is agonized over it! And here you are, months of recuperation behind and ahead of you and you're just, well, you're the same old Henry."

"Bernice—" Henry started. Then he took a deep breath, let it out, and laid back on his pillows. "Bernice, I'm not really the same old Henry. None of us guys are the same. You're changed out there. You're changed on the outside and changed on the inside."

"But Henry, you're so good-natured."

"Maybe it's because I've met God."

Bernice was startled by the abruptness of the suggestion. "What do you mean?"

Henry smiled. "I don't mean in any mystical way, or maybe, but not like Moses and the burning bush or anything. I just mean I'm one of the lucky ones who was brought up to know about God."

"Well the guy I'm thinking of, he knows about God. In fact, he and his fiancé are both very religious people."

"I don't know his circumstances, Bern, but there's something I can tell you that might help you understand mine, in particular I mean."

"Oh Henry, I don't know if I want to hear any more specifics about—"

Henry chuckled. "No, that's not what I mean. Don't worry. No replays of the battlefield today."

Bernice handed him his glass of water from the table. "Have some of this."

After he drank, Henry related the experience he had had of meeting a very special person. "After I got hit, they patched me as best they could. As I told you before, it was Sly and Harry and another guy who got me clear of the danger zone. Once I was in the hospital in London, and I'd started to see straight again, I was able to relate to the Sisters there. They're called Church of England or Anglican, but they reminded me a lot of our Sisters at St. Benedict's. Some were funny and always cheerful. Some were very quiet, like stealthy little angels in blue habits that were just suddenly there when you needed them. Some were very reverent. But they were all respectful, helpful, caring, and full of the spirit of God. Nurses are always important, but what these women gave was what made recovery possible.

You could see that they knew we needed that support, not just the medical, but the emotional and spiritual.

"It's the nurses that made the difference. I don't know where your friend's fiancé was treated, but it could be there were circumstances that made him feel bad, you know, emotionally."

"Like what?"

"Like he saw a buddy get killed, or he killed somebody at close range. All kinds of things could send someone into a depression like that."

"Depression, yeah. That sounds like it."

"Besides," said Henry, "he ain't got you!" He winked.

Bernice made a face. "Okay, now you get your treats."

Moments later, she returned with a plate of liverwurst and cheese sandwiches and a glass of milk. "If you eat this, you can have the little cakes I brought," she said.

"How did you get cakes? The grocery store?"

"Annie sent them," Bernice said with emphasis. "She also sends her best wishes."

"Good old Annie," Henry said. "How's she doing?"

"She'd be doing a lot better if she knew where her fiancé is."

Henry shook his head. "Yeah, that's rough. But she's gotta know that man is like a ninja—"

"A *what?*"

"A ninja, one of them guys that seems to be able to show up, do their thing, and then disappear into the weeds. I'll never get over how he and Bobby, his buddy, got me through them caves."

"Was it dangerous?"

Henry snorted. "Every little turn, you didn't know who or what was gonna come out at ya—was it enemy or friendly? You didn't know ''til you were right on top of 'em!"

"Okay, okay," Bernice held up her hand. "I don't wanna know no more."

"All right, I'm just saying them guys. . ." he shook his head again. "Well, tell Annie don't be worrying about old Sly. He's a superior field warrior."

"Hmph. I'll tell her don't worry. I don't know about saying anything about superior field warrior."

"Yeah on second thought," Henry laughed. "Maybe not."

"Up to this point, I thought she was nuts to worry about him. He's a translator, for crying out loud. He ain't supposed to be in the battles."

"He was assigned that way, but their work isn't regular. They don't always have somebody to rake over the coals."

"Henry!"

"Sorry. But what I mean is them guys, him and Bobby, they got the battle spirit, and they wanna help."

"I ain't telling her that either!"

"Just tell her he's the smartest, fastest guy I ever seen and there ain't no way no Nazis are gonna mess with him."

"That, I'll tell her."

"Good, now let me have my little cakes."

"I will. But I'm still waiting to hear about that very special person."

About 3400 miles away, while Bernice stood in Henry's kitchen slicing his dessert, Sly was coming to at the edge of a dangerous stretch of Italian woods. It was dark again. Sly reckoned he'd slept nine and a half hours. The sky was clear, and the rain had stopped. Both conditions were unwelcome. Whoever had shot at them once would surely try again, now that it was dark again. And whoever had shot at them before would now have the benefit of the light of a half moon.

Sly's head was throbbing, but he still had muscle control. That was a good sign, because it meant somehow the bleeding must have stopped. Bobby was breathing regularly but his temperature still seemed very high to the touch. During the night, Sly had managed to gain a share of the wagon for himself, leaving his bleeding leg inside, and good leg resting over the edge, the knee just above the ground. It turned out to be a blessing.

As he tried to stand, he felt the injured leg stripped from the khaki pant leg. Stifling a yell, he imagined suddenly the face of Jesus as his garments had been stripped from him. It was only a flash of a vision. But following it, he was left with unusual strength in that leg, and the realization that it had completely stopped bleeding.

Still in wonder at the apparent miracle, while he sat at the edge of wagon to examine his leg, he heard crackling in the woods. It was nearby.

"Not this time," he said softly. In seconds he had his rifle poised, head down, body prone. No one would fool him this time.

He could smell the wet wood, feel the icy water on the ground through his shirt. The hair was standing on end at the back of his skull.

Just then Bobby started to move. Quickly Sly was on him, hand to his mouth whispering, "Bobby, silent.

Silent." He dared not make any gestures, and because he and Bobby were so close to the ground, his actions could not be seen more than a few feet away.

Bobby seemed to understand. He stopped moving and lay still, eyes closed.

Sly flashed back to training, remembering not to whisper any words ending in the letter "s" to prevent the sound from traveling. What else, what else? He tried to think. Stay still, keep quiet, keep watch. That's it.

But as the minutes passed excruciatingly slowly, there was nothing to watch. The wood and sky remained motionless, intact, and silent. Still, he waited, concealed uncomfortably but safely.

He felt a slight breeze. Was it a true breeze or had someone walked by, he wondered. Then he chastised himself. If someone had walked by that closely, I would have seen them, certainly heard them.

He let himself breathe a little more easily but did nothing to loosen his grip on the rifle, praying that it would not jam up. Don't think about that, he commanded himself. If it does, you can't do anything about it.

After another minute, he thought he heard the slightest crack, a tiny stick or maybe it was the crack of the heavy stem of a leaf. A leaf? How could a leaf crack when it's been raining for days? No, he told himself, it was either his imagination or he was about to lose consciousness to another dream. No, no, no, I'm not doing that. That's not allowed. I won't. Bobby. There's somebody else. Don't give up, stay awake.

In his diminished state, he silently giggled, remembering a highway sign. Don't drink and drive,

Stay awake. Okay, I won't drink, he thought. No drinking. Driving, but no drinking.

Then he heard it. A serious crunch of sticks in the woods. Neither thinking, nor rising from his position, he yelled out, "Stay where you are!"

One beat later, a small voice came from the woods about 20 feet away, calling "I canna, I canna!" True to his word, the man fell out of a tree. "Io sono Batista," he said. "Imma good, Imma lover."

"Stand up! Show yourself, hands up!" Sly commanded, rising awkwardly and pointing his rifle.

Batista stood, all of about four and one-half feet tall. His hands were raised. Because of the moonlight, as Sly stood, he could scan the woods around the man. He was looking for others or even guns, but he didn't see anything.

"All right turn around," he said to Batista.

Batista complied.

Sly limped forward, pulling Bobby along in the wagon.

"Sono amico," Batista said, "Imma lover."

Sly ignored Batista's poor English, and after frisking him, removing a pistol, and determining that he was alone, Sly told him to turn back around and identify himself.

"Land uh eh. . .," Batista said.

"I speak Italian," Sly said.

"Ah! Io sono Batista, Io sono amico, per tutti."

"Per tutti?"

"No, per tutti Americani."

Sly sighed. "Perché mi hai sparato? Why did you shoot me?"

Batista scoffed. "Era mio figlio. È un idiota."

"Your son! He coulda killed me!"

"Mi ha detta che stava cacciando nazisti. Idiota."

Sly heard a cough from the wagon. He shook his head and motioned for the farmer to lead the way.

Bobby coughed again and Sly turned to look at him, alarmed. Bobby motioned him to get closer so he could speak.

"What is it, Bobby? You okay?"

Bobby nodded. Then he whispered in a raspy voice, "Don't you want a couple minutes wicher lover?"

Sly wasn't sure if he had heard correctly until he saw Bobby twitching slightly with laughter.

The farmer's wife immediately took charge of Bobby, commanding her son to carry him to the bedroom with the fireplace. Batista assisted Sly, investigating and bandaging the wound. Seeing that that bullet had hit a blood vessel, he wondered at Sly's survival.

"Come può essere? Dovresti essere morto ormai. Deve essere un miracolo da Dio."

How did you ever survive this wound?

"Si deve essere un miracolo, yes, it has to be a miracle," Sly murmured as his head rested on the farmer's shoulder. He fell instantly into a deep sleep.

Chapter Fifteen

Back in Abbottsville, Helen turned on the kettle for tea. "It's getting dark already," she called to Joan in the next room. "Better get those curtains." Helen adjusted the kitchen curtains so that no light would radiate out from inside the house.

Joan did the same with the curtains in the living room. The light inside the houses could give enemy aircraft a good reckoning, or idea, where and what to target. For that reason, citizens were required to keep blackout or solid, non-light-emitting covers on all windows at night when the lights were switched on.

"Got them," Joan called. "Days are sure getting short, aren't they?"

"Yes," said Helen entering the dining room. "Oh doesn't that table look pretty! It's nice that we can dress it up from time to time, for no real reason."

Joan nodded. "It helps, Helen, don't you think? I mean with it getting cold, dark, and everything else, here's a beautiful table with your Irish linen tablecloth, beautiful floral china and embroidered napkins. It's like an oasis of happiness."

"Let's sit a while before the others get here," Helen said. "We haven't had a chance to chat in a long time."

"I know. I thought with no job, I'd be over here all the time. I didn't count on all the volunteer work at the church. Not that I'm complaining."

"No, me either," said Helen. "What would we do if we didn't have all of this to keep us busy? Just be sitting around worrying all the time."

"We've sure given Faith a run for its money!" Joan said.

"Boy, haven't we! The heartache could have gone either way. Turned to anger and bitterness or stayed strong in heart and soul. We're lucky."

"We are," Joan agreed.

"Have you seen your friend Laureen lately?"

"No, but I know she's planning to try to make another visit to the hospital and wants me to come. Bob remains adamant against her visiting. She doesn't care. She's desperate, Helen. I think after talking to Father Bertrand, she understood a little, but the situation is really boiling up. I don't know how much longer she'll hang on.

"Father told her that there is a kind of guilt that the men feel, the ones who survive. If they don't accept that they are actually here for a reason, or survived for a reason, they feel they should have died along with the others."

"Did Bob lose friends?"

"I know there were men in his Company that died," Joan said. "Being wounded, and pretty seriously, I thought he wouldn't be as prone to the guilt, but maybe it's more because of. . ." Joan's voice trailed off.

"He really doesn't *know* anything," Helen said quickly, sensing that Joan's thoughts were on Dick.

"No, about Dick? No. He only knows what he heard. And Helen, he's sick, you know. He has been on strong pain medication. Father said he could easily have missed a lot, just been asleep when the details of Dick's treatment and progress were discussed."

"That's so true. Father had his own harrowing experiences in earlier wars, you know, so he's no stranger to the emotional tangles that grab hold of these men. And then, too, spending time with these fellows myself has made me keenly aware of the pain they're in and how much of their time is spent either sleeping or just dopey."

Joan giggled. "I've always liked that word, dopey."

Just then the door opened, and Bernice stuck her head inside. "Anybody home?"

"Hey, what do you know?" Joan said. "She heard us calling her name."

Helen giggled. "Hello, dear," she said. "Annie with you?"

"Yep," called Annie from the steps. "I'm comin'. She left me the heavy stuff to carry."

"Darn right," said Bernice. "And what do you mean, I heard my name?"

"Nothing," said Joan, smiling. "What have you got, Annie, that's so heavy?"

"Ma dropped some'n off," she said, crossing through to the kitchen and placing two heavy pastry boxes onto the table. "Let me put it down. Part of it's for us, part for the priests."

"Whatever it is, thank you!" Joan said.

"Goes double for me," said Helen. "I couldn't get my sugar ration this week—every single grocery store was clean out!"

"They probably gave it to their bakery," Annie said, laughing. "Seriously though, they're not watching what these commercial places order. Maybe I can get us a few pounds, especially if you're not getting even your ration filled."

"When we get closer to Christmas, I might just ask you to do that!" Helen said. "I think the reason everyone's rushing to have it is because they're all baking ahead of time and putting their sweet goodies away for the holidays."

Sugar had to be rationed, or carefully portioned out to each household because of shortages of it during the war. Only a few pounds per person per week were allowed, and in order to buy that, the shopper must have his or her ration ticket for that item. But the store could only sell it if it had not run out of supplies. Even Bernice's little grocery store wasn't able to keep up with the rationed demand.

"We're having trouble, too," Bernice said. "It's tough being the new kid on the block. They try to take advantage of my lack of experience, and they're doing a good job. I've really got to get a decent manager, a guy who knows business or accounting or something. I really just don't know that much about the business. I guess there's not too many businessmen floating around."

The girls were all quiet for a moment, thinking similar thoughts. Finally Annie said, "Not too many *any* guys around right now."

"Ah, they'd just mess up everything anyway," Joan said, smiling sadly.

"Yeah, probably eat up all the food before we got any ourselves," Annie joined in.

Helen smiled. "That's the spirit, girls," she said nodding. "We'll get through this."

The plan was to share dinner together first, and afterward, talk about the idea Bernice wanted to explore. She wanted to use a portion of her inheritance to start a school for art, music, and theatre students. She had written some notes but lacked direction on the project.

"I think I'm losing my oomph," Annie said after a couple of hours at the job. "I keep reading this same sentence over and over again."

"Well, I'm glad it's not just me," said Helen. "I thought maybe age was finally catching up with me."

"Well we've made a little progress," Bernice said, closing her big planning binder.

"I know we have good ideas," Joan said. "But do you think we're the right people to help you plan this? We don't have any experience at all in running a school."

"I know it," Bernice said. "As we were talking about dates and testing, I realized my idea might be a little bit too ambitious. It's okay, I'm not crushed."

"We can certainly have classes in music, art, and maybe drama, too," said Helen, "as well as things we all already do, like sewing, crafts, baking. What do you think about that?"

"I was thinking the same thing," Bernice answered. We could use maybe a building that's already there, start small and see how it goes."

"I love that idea!" Joan said. "I would love to teach whatever you think I'm capable of."

"Well I'm pooped," said Annie. "I throw my hat in there, too. But for tonight, I better start walking before I fall asleep in my chair."

"That cold air will wake you up!" Joan nudged her.

On the way home, just as Joan was about to ask Annie for a Lifesaver, Annie gasped.

"Joan look!"

The two girls froze. Beyond the line of houses and up on the ocean horizon they spotted the single circle of orangey yellow light, signifying the presence of a vessel.

"What is that?" Joan whispered.

"It ain't no Navy ship, I can tell you that," Annie said. "That's a no-sail zone."

"What do we do?"

Annie's heart was beating rapidly. She tried to remember what Sly had said, wishing so hard that she had paid better attention. "Okay, I think we wait and watch, to see what it does. If it circles and then kind of sinks, we're in trouble," she said, her voice shaking.

Joan clutched her arm.

They stood in silence watching as the light traveled slowly up the coast. Then it appeared to come to a standstill.

"Do you think they spotted us?" Joan asked, choking on her words.

"Don't be silly," Annie whispered. "They can't see us. We're in the dark. In fact, why are we whispering?"

As they continued to watch, the light turned eastward, away from the shore and slowly disappeared, but didn't sink.

Joan and Annie looked at each other wide-eyed, then instantly took off down the block.

As they tore through the door, Annie puffed, "I think we're supposed to call someone."

"The civil people?" Joan asked.

"Well, uh, yeah, oh, what is it called. . ." Annie slapped her hand repeatedly on the table thinking.

"The Civil Defense!" Joan said.

"That's it!"

"Well, where do they live?"

"Gosh, I don't know. I don't know if they live somewhere or they have an office."

"Helen would know!"

"Yeah, let's call Helen."

Moments later, Helen was on the phone giving them the number. "Let me know what they say," she said.

As Annie dialed, her hands were shaking. "Here," she said, "you talk to them."

"Why me?" said Joan.

"'Cause I'm shaking," Annie said. "They're libel to think I'm a quack."

"Well I don't know what to say," Joan said, taking the receiver. "Oh! Hello? Oh yes, this is Joan. I'm calling because Annie and I saw a light."

Annie made a face. "Give me the phone."

"Could you repeat that?" she heard a man's voice say.

"I'm sorry, Sir. We're calling to report sighting a vessel in the no-sail zone, Abbotsville. . . Yes, just now. No. It didn't submerge. It turned and appeared to go directly away from shore. Yeah, east, I guess. . . Okay. Thank you."

"What'd he say?" Joan asked as she hung up the phone. "I'm glad you took it. I was so flustered."

"I know. He said they were going to alert somebody. Some master or something."

"Master?"

"I can't remember, but he said thank you and then hung up."

They both let out a sigh. "Joanie, that was creepy," Annie said. "I could feel the hairs on my arms standing up."

"Do you think it was Germans?"

"I don't know."

Suddenly they heard the sound of a helicopter overhead. It seemed to have appeared instantly in place above their house. It moved rapidly out toward the ocean. The power of the engine filled the girls, and probably most of the neighbors, with awe. They could even hear the sound of rotors.

"How in the world did they get here so fast?" Joan breathed. "We just called!"

"Maybe someone else saw it."

"Yeah, the local guy who's always wearing that uniform."

"Or maybe someone else taking a walk, like we were."

Not being allowed to peep through the window because of the blackout rules, they were unable to see the path the helicopter took.

"That's the same thing they used up in Sandy Hook, you know," Annie said. "To get the wounded to the hospital."

"No kidding," said Joan. "I'm still shaking."

"Yeah, me too. Let's make some tea and sit for a while. I bet we never find out what it was we saw."

"I bet you're right," Joan said.

The girls filled in Helen and Bernice the next day, but they would never know that what they had seen was a light reconnaissance craft deployed by Germany.

Its mission had been to scout dense population areas along the East Coast of the United States. While making a hasty retreat, it was greeted with a rapid US Navy craft who made quick work of the German crew, taking all five prisoner. The craft was then returned to the shore and examined to provide intel to the Navy.

Chapter Sixteen

A crispy chill rippled through the neighborhood as December advanced. Helen buzzed around her living room, dusting, picking up magazines, and rearranging the candy dishes and scented rosebud bon bons on the end tables.

In fact, her house was remarkably spotless. Bernice called it "the White House." Its immaculate condition was largely a testament to the philosophy that busy hands were happy hands.

"It just can't go on forever," Helen said to no one in particular. "It has to end sometime."

She carried a vase into the kitchen to clean it out. Harry had bought it for her when they had visited a glass blower's shop in Pennsylvania. It was a swirly blue and transparent glass, with unusually thick walls for something blown. Many months had passed since it had seen any flowers, but Helen liked to have it in her living room for sentimental reasons. It was also a thing of beauty. But she disdained fingerprints on anything.

As she dried it, she heard a knock on the door. "Just me!" called Joan. "You busy?"

"Busying myself," Helen called back. "Come on in."

"I can't stay," Joan said. "I was just on my way to Laureen's house."

"So you have decided to accompany her?"

"On her quest to reunite with her fiancé? Yes. I have to admit I am a little nervous about it."

"Well, if she's determined, I guess there's no stopping her. It does seem like he's taking the hard-to-get routine a little far."

Joan smiled and nodded and took a seat on the couch. "Don't you wish it were that simple! I think she just needs to see him, to know one way or the other how things will go. It's been so long already, and she doesn't want to be waiting for a man who isn't going to come back."

"Yes," Helen said, joining her on the sofa. "That does make sense. I just hope it doesn't go against her." She studied her hands.

"Me, too," said Joan. "I'm going because if everything's fine, I can just walk around the hospital while they visit. But if it goes badly, I'll be there for her."

"You'll be the shock absorber."

"Yeah, I guess you could say that. What are you up to today?"

"Straightening up, and then I thought I'd work on a few shell creations for the bazaar. I know it's coming up really soon, but I've got some time and I feel like getting my hands on something and creating today."

"To tell you the truth, I'd rather be joining you than going off on this mission of mercy," Joan said smiling as she stood up.

"I wish you the best! If it doesn't seem like things are going well, look around the room and make sure you find something to duck behind."

Joan giggled. "Okay, I'll do that," she said.

As Helen closed the door, Joan wished again that she were on the other side, setting up the tea things and getting ready for a designing session with the girls. But Laureen was her friend, too, and there were things that friends had to do, times when they needed to be there for each other. This was one of those times.

Covering the distance to Laureen's house, Joan grew more nervous. The task ahead was a little daunting. Laureen had always been the one to work things out, helping Joan in so many ways to meet and then get to know Dick. This would be Joan's opportunity to return the favor. But what if Joan didn't have the same ability? And somewhere inside, she simply did not feel confident that it was the right move for Laureen to make. Of course, it's not my relationship, she told herself, and who knows best about it but Bob and Laureen?

When she got to Laureen's house, there was her friend, on her front stoop waiting for her, looking very cheerful. "Hey, right on time!" she called.

"Are you ready for this?" Joan asked.

"Yep," was all Laureen said.

They walked in silence to the corner and crossed the street just as the bus to Atlantic City pulled up.

The bus ride brought back memories for Joan of going to work in the early mornings. She had caught the bus further down the street each day to her secretarial job. As the war wore on, her company had less and less business and she had been let go. But the clickity clank of the bus, the sound of the change bouncing around, and the frequent bumps along the road reminded her of better times.

What will it be like to be able to go to the store again, she wondered, to have enough to buy what I want and have the products I want actually be present in the store?

She gave Laureen a smile. Instantly she felt guilty. What am I worrying about, she thought. Food and goodies while Laureen is going through the fight of her life.

Laureen smiled back, as if she could read Joan's thoughts. "Neither of us is doing all that great right now," she said. "But Joanie, if I don't do this today, I think I will burst!"

Joan nodded. "You gotta do what you feel is right."

"That's right," said Laureen resolutely. "Mom thought I should wait, and I don't know what Dad thought. But I just can't sit around and wonder anymore. Suppose Bob says, well, the real reason is I met someone else? Then why should I wait? I'll just be getting older waiting around for something that will never be!"

"Oh Laureen—I can see how you might worry about that, but it will *never happen!*"

"You know, Joan, a few months ago, even *one* month ago, I would have agreed with you no problem. But now, all this waiting, all this stalling around it feels like. I just don't know. That's one of the really bad parts of this—it's making me actually doubt Bob." Laureen shook her head, sighed, and looked out the window.

The bus bumped along. Joan was sure Laureen was mistaken. But what if she wasn't? What if all the fun and games was because Bob had met another girl and didn't know how to break it to Laureen? She reviewed what she remembered of the recent past.

Laureen had met up with her after many years at the very dance where she had met Dick Thimble. Joan drew in her breath suddenly at the thought of that dance. Dick was so handsome and had a quality about him that just made her tune into him completely. Then, as the dark shadow of doubt in her own mind about Dick's survival started to creep in, she shook it off.

That's it, Joan thought. The very same doubts are plaguing us both. Suddenly she felt strong, involuntarily grasping the Miraculous Medal that hung on a chain around her neck. "Listen, Laureen," she said. "We've both got reason to doubt, but let's throw it all out the window. Let's just put our best foots forward—"

Laureen giggled. "Our best *foots?*" she said.

But Joan was not to be dissuaded. "Yes, our best foots. And if we don't meet with the best outcomes, we'll find happiness somewhere else!"

Laureen couldn't help but catch the energy her friend was sharing. She bumped her with her shoulder, nodding. "Okay," she said. "All for one and one for all."

Entering the hospital, Joan looked around, trying to remember the old convention hall and the things that had been replaced by either soldiers or military supplies, machines, or equipment. It was a shock. Still, the hospital was not a cold one and the fellow coming towards them looked friendly enough.

"Are you here to see Father Bertrand this morning?" he asked Laureen.

Joan was startled, but said nothing.

"Yes, can you take us?" Laureen answered.

"Sure, just give me a minute," said the soldier.

"Father Bertrand?" whispered Joan. "What's he talking about?"

"Shhh!" Laureen whispered back. "That's how I get in here. They think I work for him."

Joan felt a shiver down her spine. The idea of lying to get in to see someone who had expressed a desire not to be seen seemed perilous, ill-advised at the very least.

As they followed the young soldier down the long hallways and upstairs, Joan could see Laureen's determination beginning to wane.

"Looks like Father's visiting Luigi Mazza," the soldier said, peering into a room. "You'd better wait here. I think they're having Confession."

"Okay, we will," said Laureen.

After the soldier had left to return to his post, Laureen turned and stood with her back against the wall. Her face was pale.

Joan sighed and shook her head. "Is Bob rooming with Mr. Mazza?"

Laureen chuckled nervously. "No, he's down the hall, two more rooms."

"What are you going to do?" Joan had begun to whisper.

Laureen made a face. "I'm scared. But Joanie, I gotta. . ."

"Maybe you're changing your mind. That's okay." That's *better*, thought Joan.

"No. Come on."

"Wait! Don't go in mad. You haven't seen him in months! Go in smiling, happy."

Laureen turned and gave Joan a smile, albeit a limp one, and pulled her by the arm. As they approached Bob's room, Joan took a deep breath and let it out. Okay, here goes, she thought.

When they entered, Bob appeared to be sleeping, facing away from them.

Joan and Laureen exchanged glances. They moved a little closer, unsure of what to say.

As they approached, Joan could see Bob's leg, slightly elevated, thickly bandaged just above and below the knee. But his foot had on a regular enough looking sock, and there was no visible blood. Hmm, not so bad, she thought. He must be coming along well.

But Laureen was looking only at the back of Bob's head. She could all but feel his thick hair between her fingers and smell the scent of his cologne. The sight of the two of them walking the Atlantic City boardwalk flashed through her mind. Before she could stop herself, she said, "It's been a long time, soldier."

Joan froze.

Bob's head lifted, and slowly he moved his bandaged leg down onto the bed and turned his body to face them. He had only a hospital gown on, its short sleeves revealing two intravenous lines. One of them was attached to a stand with two bottles, running into his left forearm. The other was closer to his wrist, and attached to a stand with a bottle dripping into a fluid in the tube below it.

His body seemed very thin through the gown, and his movements were labored. But it was his face that told the story. Joan could see the humiliation he felt in his eyes. Instinctively, she turned away.

But Laureen was not aware, and rushed toward him, embracing him gently but warmly. "Oh Bob, it's been so long! I'm sorry I came before you wanted me, but I just had to see you. I just had to feel your arms around me."

Bob was in fact putting his arms around her the best he could, but his facial expression had not changed.

"You look so much better than I expected," Laureen went on. "You've only got the one bandage. I bet you can even walk on it by now, can't you, dear?" As she spoke she started to reach for his leg.

Quickly and a little too sharply Bob grabbed her hand. "No," he said hoarsely. "You can't touch it."

It was then that Laureen noticed that Bob was not enthusiastic to see her. "I'm sorry," she said. She turned to look at Joan, who was edging toward the door.

"I'll leave you to your visit," Joan said. "Hello, Bob. I'll come back a little later."

Bob looked at her briefly, nodded, and then sighed heavily.

Laureen bit her lip. "I know you said not to come—"

"That's right," said Bob flatly.

Laureen swallowed. "Yes, well, Bob, it's been so long and I," she paused to think of what to say. Why didn't I plan what I would say, she thought. Her thoughts and feelings were muddled. She had been prepared for him to be upset, but she had not anticipated the coldness. "I just had to see you, honey. That's . . . all."

"I left word with Mrs. Ashenbach that I did not want anyone to come yet," Bob said. "Didn't she say anything to you?"

"Well, yes, she did, and as I say, I knew that, but I—"

"This isn't high school," Bob said. "It's serious. It's life."

Laureen was beginning to panic. Who *was* this man? Where had the warm, funny, always loving Bob gone? The more she thought, the greater she panicked. She felt a little bit outside of her own body, the way she had when years before she had had rheumatic fever.

She pulled back, trying to steady herself, looking around for something to lean on other than Bob. She was unaware of the tears that had begun to frost her eyes.

Turning her back, she pretended to be doing something with her shoe while she tried to figure out what to say. She took a deep breath, then let it out. Okay, she thought. Just try to get a hold of yourself.

"I know it's not high school, Bob," she said, her voice shaking. "I didn't expect you to be in your football uniform. And I knew you were injured. I've always been good with injured people, or pets, or anything. I thought," she gulped as the tears began to flow. "I thought I could help."

Bob studied her, his head tilting to the side. "They help me here," he said. "They see to all the soldiers who come through here."

Laureen stood awkwardly, looking for a handkerchief. Only a year ago, she thought, this very same man would have knocked himself out to give me his handkerchief. Finally she found one and wiped her eyes. She stared at him as he stared back, seemingly softening but nowhere near the man she had said goodbye to only a year before. "Don't you," she stopped, unsuccessfully fighting the tears. Her voice dropped to a husky whisper, "Don't you love me anymore at all?"

Bob drew in his breath, "Laureen," he said.

Laureen felt a deep pang at his saying her name. She began to cry openly.

"I don't know anything," Bob said. "I still need time."

Laureen caught her breath and leaned back against the wall to gather her strength. She was disappointed in herself for falling apart this way. If Bob didn't know, then for heaven's sakes, why was she suffering so much over him? She wanted to be strong, but her heart was breaking. "If you loved me," she said through the mist, "you would know."

She turned and quickly left the room to hide her agonized sobs. But they echoed through the hall, increasing her embarrassment, but she could not stop.

Joan quickly put her arms around her and let her cry as long as she wanted.

Bob could not help but hear. Through the wall that had become his world, he could still feel her pain. A tear rolled hotly down his face, landing on the IV tubing attached at his wrist. Like a heartbeat, the tear brought him hope. But still so inside of his guilt and shame, he felt powerless to pursue it. He returned to his previous position and tried to go back to the dark sleep where he had been only moments before.

Chapter Seventeen

That same morning, as Laureen cried bitter tears, Bernice was starting to worry about something she had thought would never again be a concern.

"What does it mean?" Henry asked, tapping the envelope. Henry had improved as expected and was now allowed to sit up for periods of time.

"I will have to call the lawyers," Bernice answered. "But I doubt there's any problem. It could be Uncle Louie just being funny again. He was confusing to me when I was younger. And this might just be more of the same."

"Yeah, who knows what a letter means. You can doublecheck with the lawyers to be sure, but it's probably just him musing about things."

Bernice was mildly comforted by his words, but her uncle's letter, neatly concealed in a book he had left her, had her worried. He had written:

As you will soon discover, there are many things due, or coming due, that I pay every year. Don't let that bother you, my dear. There should still be quite enough for you and your mother for many years to come. But be sure to have old Wheeler sell off those trouble spots so you won't be paying for them every year.

"I think you're right, I hope you're right," Bernice said as she went to make some tea. "Brrr, it's chilly! Are you warm enough?"

"Yes, I'm fine," said Henry. "Any time I start to think of complaining, I think of that super old fellow at the hospital."

"You never told me about him," Bernice called from the kitchen. "Is he the special person you mentioned before?"

"Yes. Really special. In fact, if it had not been for him, I might not have come home in such a great mood!" Henry called back to her. "So you are lucky."

Bernice chuckled, returning to his room. "The water will take a few minutes to heat. And yes, I am lucky. There sure have been casualties with this war. Some seen, some unseen."

"That's one of the things this old guy told me," Henry went on. "It's the unseen ones that linger, and tear at your heart if you don't route them out. You know how you do it?"

"Do what?" Bernice said, smoothing her dress and sitting down.

"Route out the evil."

"I'd sure like to know!"

"One word. Forgiveness."

"Forgiveness? Forgive the Nazis?" Bernice's eyes were wide. It was a suggestion she had not heard before.

"Maybe. Maybe it makes all the difference. They're going to lose this war, Bernice. They're splintering now, just like all evil forces eventually do. And when we're victorious, we'll be able to see what hatred does. It makes men crazy."

"That's pretty heavy stuff for a night runner," Bernice said.

"Sprinter!" Henry laughed. "But I like your name better."

"Sprinter," said Bernice.

"And it's not coming from me, by the way. Let me tell you about this old man. He's a man of God, a foreigner."

Bernice giggled. "Foreigner? Seems like you were the foreigner."

"Uh, well, yeah, I guess so," Henry laughed again. "But he aint from here anyway. Bern, he was from one of them countries where they got persecuted, and got persecuted really bad. I mean this guy was literally running for his life."

"Well how old is he that he could still run?"

"Listen Bernice, when it's your life, you can run, no matter how old you are. He had some people hidden, him and this other guy."

"Another foreigner?"

"Seriously Bernice. No kidding, this is really something. He was running from Nazis, hiding in old shelled out buildings, trying to keep other people safe. Until one day, the guys caught on that he was one of the guys helping and they put him on the list, or something like that. He was shot at twice, and then taken prisoner. They missed him with the bullets, but they don't spare the rod, if you know what I mean, in the prisons. Even for frail old guys."

"That's horrible. And he lived through all of that?" Bernice was startled by the up-close recounting of the man's story. It was different and far more overwhelming than simply reading war statistics in the newspaper.

"That's only the first half of his story. Then there was a riot, some kind of uprising in that part of Poland, and the rioters broke open the prison."

"Was he Polish?"

"No, one of the guys was, one of the other clergy. But he was something else, I can't remember. Anyway, he helped a bunch of folks get out and then this truck come and picked up his tired body and brought him to a safe house. Well, it wasn't safe for long, and he and a bunch of the others were captured again, and that time, they about did him in."

"He was a priest?"

"Yeah, a priest or one of the religious. I never found out for sure. Well, the same Polish priest somehow managed to get him out, and got him onto a rescue boat, kind of like the one I was on, but faster, and had him sent to the hospital where I was, over in England.

"Bernice, when I say he was starving, I mean there was nothing to this guy. He was like a ghost. You could see through his skin. What veins he had that had not collapsed were so tiny it was like looking at spiderwebs or something. They had trouble moving him because if he were to get another bruise, it might actually mean the end of his life."

Bernice sighed. "Any time I start to complain, Lord let me remember him."

"If there was anybody who had a right to complain, it was this guy. And I remember telling him what a rotten, miserable sack of, well, garbage the Germans are. Bernice, you wouldn't believe what he said to me. He says if you don't forgive, you will never be free.

And I was angry. I was real angry, them guys shooting my guts out like that—oh sorry. But I got the royal treatment. This guy?" Henry shook his head. "I have to stop myself, getting all choked up. There he was, miraculously recovering, having tea and then a nutritional drink, and eventually actually eating food and gaining weight, but with the most peaceful and kind of saintly attitude."

Henry paused to sip the tea that Bernice had brought.

"And it stayed with you," Bernice said. "That's a testament right there."

Henry looked serious for a moment. "Oh, it ain't *ever* gonna leave me. I can tell you that for sure. He changed me. I went from hating them damn Nazis to just putting them behind me and using my brain to survive, not wasting any energy on anger. He said if you don't leave it behind, you're a prisoner of it. And he's right."

"Maybe that's part of what's bothering Bob," Bernice mused. "Maybe he's got some stored-up hatred."

"It could be," Henry said, "but it sounds more like he's got battlefield guilt. He survived and others died. That really messes with you."

"So I've got this wonderful man to thank for you coming back healthy in mind," Bernice squeezed his hand as a tear rolled down her cheek.

Henry smiled. "He inspired me to change. I figured if he could do it, I certainly could. I wonder how he made out. Last I heard, he was discharged and healthy. But he sure wasn't going back home."

"Well if I ever meet him," Bernice snuffed, "I'll have some hugs for him."

After Henry went to sleep, Bernice took out Uncle Louie's letter again. What worried her was the fact that because she had acted so quickly, her beloved Order, the Benedictines, had already moved into the new building that her uncle had left her. What if that building were one of the "old trouble spots" that he had indicated needed to be sold? It was in the process of being renovated for the nuns. Maybe tonight Helen will have some suggestions, she thought.

The plan had been that the building would become the Sisters' permanent residence, and that Bernice's investment would provide them enough income to maintain themselves and the building permanently. If it were problematic and would mean that Bernice could not provide them an income, especially when she herself hoped to be one of the residents one day, what would she do?

For the hundredth time, she found herself wishing she had gained more knowledge before having received the fortune. The inheritance had been unforeseen though, and like so many things, had to be squeezed into one's life, whether welcome or not.

That evening, sharing time together at Helen's house, the girls were less enthusiastic than any of them could remember. The darkening sky in the afternoon had brought a wild storm during dinner which had threatened to shut off the lights several times before blowing out to the Atlantic.

Assembled around the table, striving to be joyful, but failing, the four women decided to pray a decade of the rosary for peace. At the end, Helen stood up to clear the dishes.

"I may be making too big of a thing, but I just thought I would have heard from Harry by now. I'm only gloomy out of impatience. I get the feeling the rest of you have a lot more on your minds."

"Not really," said Annie, who had arrived late from the shop. "I'm having trouble with the lights in the shop, but that's nothing new. And all I think about when I'm alone is where is Sylvester? How is he, etc. etc. and I'm sure everyone here is tired of hearing it."

"I'm never tired of hearing it, Annie," Joan said. "I honestly wish I had gone with you to work today instead of accompanying Laureen, though."

"Why? What happened?" Annie asked.

"You guys, it was a disaster," Joan said, happy to be able to recount it to them. "Remember when I stopped in Helen, and said I really didn't want to go, but thought I should? Well now I'm wondering if going encouraged Laureen to go. But whatever the case, it was a big mistake!"

"Was Bob unconscious?" Annie asked, missing the point.

"No. Well, let's put it this way. The Bob we all know and love was unconscious, and the new Bob was there instead."

Helen shook her head sadly.

"I was so embarrassed," Joan continued. "From the minute we walked in, I could tell it was a colossal mistake. And what's worse is Laureen did not realize it until they had had words."

"He yelled at her?" Annie asked, horrified.

"No, well, not really. It's more like he was just emotionless. Almost like shell shock in the movies, but in a different kind of way. I was stunned. After he spoke, I left the room. I had a feeling there might be things said in there that were not any of my business.

"Unfortunately, I could hear him from where I waited in the hall. He wasn't yelling, and Laureen wasn't either. But the hallways are wide and echoey."

"What did he say?" Annie asked.

"I can't really remember what he said, but I know that when she tried to touch his wounded leg, he caught her arm and told her not to touch him. That was right at the beginning, and it went downhill from there.

"Laureen came out of there actually balling. It was one of the most heartbreaking scenes I've ever witnessed."

"Did they break up then?" Helen asked.

"I don't know," said Joan. "I think it was left kind of in that direction, but I just don't believe it. We've all seen them together. We know how much in love they are. Bob has always been crazy about Laureen and vice versa. I have to believe that it will get better."

"Well, if I were you," said Helen, "and she asks you to go with her again, I would say no!"

Joan smiled wryly. "Good advice," she said. "I think I'll take it!"

"You've been quiet in your little corner tonight," said Annie to Bernice. "Is this the new Bernice, or did your day go just as nicely as Joan's?

"Gosh, no, it wasn't nearly that painful," Bernice answered. "But I've got stuff on my mind." Quickly she explained the problem to the girls. "So you see, I don't know what the story is and it's unsettling. I put a call in to Mr. Wheeler, and I'm waiting to hear back."

"Are you worried he won't call back?" Annie asked.

"No, why would I be worried about that?" Bernice asked.

"He might yell at you for stealing all those pastries."

Finally the girls had something to laugh about, remembering Annie and Bernice's fateful trip to Philadelphia.

"Did you really swipe *all* of the pastries?" Joan giggled.

"She stowed them right in her purse," Helen said. "Like the prudent girl that she is."

"Hey look, they offered them to us, it's not like we snuck them," Bernice said.

"Yeah we did," said Annie. "Remember how fast you got them in there?"

They all burst out laughing again.

"That was quite a day, finding out you had a wealthy uncle, but also that he'd left his fortune to you!"

"Remember we thought it was just the clock?" Annie said.

Bernice nodded, smiling at the memory. Mr. Wheeler's office had notified her that she was requested at the reading of the will. She had always admired Uncle Louie's cuckoo clock, so naturally she had assumed that was what her dear old uncle had left her. Instead she went home from Philadelphia trying to digest the fact that she had inherited millions in property and investments. But it hadn't turned out to be an easy development.

"So what do I do if the nuns' building is one of the problem properties?" Bernice asked. "How can I possibly ask them to move out right after they've just moved in?"

"Can't you just tell Mr. Wheeler, listen, I'm keeping that and I'll sell something else?" Joan asked.

"That's what I don't know. I guess there's no point in thinking about all of this before I speak to the lawyer. Maybe I should do what Henry does and put it all behind me for now."

"What Henry does?" Helen asked. "What's that?"

"We had this great discussion about a priest or some clergyman who was old and frail, a Nazi victim, but who had been rescued and was in the same hospital as Henry."

"Wow, that must have been something!"

"Yeah Annie, it really was. And Henry was struck by the man's grace and his resolution to forgive. Henry says because of their talks, he understands that you have to put the experiences behind you. If you possibly can, forgive your enemies."

Annie snorted. "Forgive them Nazis? I don't think so."

Joan sighed. "That's a tall order, Bernice, and how about the Japanese?"

"Yeah," Bernice said. "Well anyway, it worked for that man, and Henry too. "

"I think it sounds inspired. I wouldn't mind meeting that fellow," Helen said.

"Helen!" Annie said, falsely indignant. "You're a *married woman*."

Helen grimaced.

"You had to say that," Bernice said, going to Helen's side.

"No, no. No need to interrupt any levity we've got, girls," Helen shook it off. "Annie, don't give it another thought. I'm still a married woman, through and through. You got that right, and I am not worried one lick about Harry."

"No need to be," Joan said, "Harry's a tough old guy."

"And watch who you're calling 'old,'" Helen said, smiling.

"He might be old," Annie said, "but he's a good kind of old."

"Yeah, like 'Good old Harry," Bernice added.

"They're all good old guys," Helen said quietly.

Instinctively, they grabbed each other's hands, making a circle, sitting contentedly.

"Okay, enough of this," said Annie. "Who wants a cookie?"

Chapter Eighteen

Gloria Marini tidied up her make-believe medical bag. While it contained a stethoscope and first aid gear such as bandages, and applications, it was only a large yarn bag she'd bought at her boyfriend's department store.

Boyfriend, she scoffed, thinking about him. They are just good for a month or two, then they're gone. What I really need is that gorgeous soldier from last year.

What is it about Dick Thimble, she wondered. She could see him just as plainly as he was that night, if she closed her eyes. He was tall and dark-haired, a strong stature, but somehow intelligent and gentle looking. Yet so very manly.   She sighed. And there he was, wasting his efforts on that little church girl. Didn't she know high school was over? It was just a matter of time before Dick got tired of Joan Schmoan, whatever her last name was, and all her religious parading. A man wanted excitement. If Joan wanted to be a nun, she should have kept her hands off of the most eligible man at that dance.

She studied her fingernails. Not a blemish, perfectly lacquered "Peasant's Kiss" in a brilliant orangey red.

Peasant's Kiss, she thought, snorting. I should give a bottle of this to Joan!

Her right hand was endowed with a lovely but slightly ostentatious ruby ring, circled with pearls, which matched her earrings. They hung slightly off her ear in a ring of pearls with tiny diamonds in the center.

She had chosen a rich woolen, coffee-colored suit, with a silk blouse in brilliant white, dazzled with large pearly buttons and a line of pearls at the edges of the collar. Her shoes were a coffee colored Italian leather, bought one year before the war, but still perfectly buffed, featuring a small circle of brass at the outside end of the straps.

She was proud of her appearance and of her father's large income, and she wore them both very well. On that day, though, she'd suffered a slight embarrassment when arriving for training.

It was Gloria's wish to take a position that would present her as a caring person, one with great compassion. She had observed Joan and Annie and, ironically, decided that their actions had made them desirable. So she entered First Aid Training I, provided by the Abbottsville Fire Company.

However, that day, she had been informed that all trainees were to arrive in tennis shoes and easy dress, not accessorized and no heels; that the job was a physical one that heels would simply fail to accommodate. She was asked to wear a used pair of tennis shoes left there by donation, and remove her jewelry.

The others who had dressed appropriately were not rude, but Gloria was sure they were laughing to themselves. They're nowhere near as pretty as me, she told herself. Jealous is all.

Nevertheless, after the first session, the instructor reminded her to dress appropriately the following day. She smiled at the older man sweetly, as she put on her plush winter coat, but privately thought dark thoughts.

It was in that frame of mind that Gloria came upon Joan on that morning.

Joan had agreed to help out that day in Annie's vespers shop, secretly hoping to find a present for her parents at a discounted price. Annie loved Joan's parents, and Joan knew that. But Annie was also pretty careful about pricing.

Annie's order for the new statues had come into the shop the previous week. In unpacking them, Joan had nearly fallen in love with a statue of St. Michael the Archangel. It was colorful, masterfully painted, his expression strong and protective against the evil Lucifer who lay slithering at his feet. The retail price was higher than she could afford, though, and if Annie would just sliver off enough, she could make it a lovely Christmas gift to her parents.

The wind was picking up as she walked down 23rd Street. She pulled the collar of her wool coat up around her neck, wishing that she had remembered her muffler. The prickly wool of her collar, pretty and warm as it was, made her neck itch. Helen's crocheted muffler had been a very much appreciated gift.

In fact, everything about Helen and all of the girls was dear to her. The previous night had been a godsend. The peace and friendship between them seemed to grow stronger with every crisis. And the prayers they shared were the durability, the bonding strength that kept them connected.

As Joan passed the diner, she wished she could stop in for at least a hot cup of coffee. But she felt in her pockets and there was not one single dime left. She quickened her pace.   Just then, she thought she recognized someone approaching further down the block. Oh dear, if that's Gloria, maybe I should turn around, she thought. After last night's wonderful feelings, I don't want the world to turn all sour. Who needs help feeling bad these days?

But as she got closer, her better nature took hold, and she decided maybe this will be the one time, when there's no one else around, that they can talk like just two girls, friendly, peaceful. Afterall, she thought, Gloria is my age, she's a girl, and she might be well-off, but she really is not that different from me. We wear different clothes, and have different interests, but we both want nice families and pretty houses.

Joan had always seen the good side of things, even if there was not really one to see. And that was her frame of mind when she came upon Gloria that day.

"Good morning, Gloria. How are you today?" Joan asked, stopping to speak. "You look so pretty."

"Well, Joan, I'm shocked. What a surprise that you have time to talk to me."

Joan opened her mouth, but couldn't find the words. Instead, she smiled meekly.

"Oh yes," Gloria went on, "I'm sure you've heard that my boyfriend and I have parted ways, and you're dying to know what happened. That's the only reason you would stoop to having conversation with someone outside of your clique."

Joan was genuinely confused. "My what? My click? What are you talking about?"

It was just about then that Bernice found herself turning the corner onto 23rd and saw the girls in conversation. That's interesting, she thought. And she continued on to get a closer look.

"Don't be sarcastic," Gloria fired at Joan, her face flushing, approaching the shade of her hair. "At least *I* take the time to look good, even when there aren't men around, and don't frump around like you, in work clothes. Where did you get that coat? Was that a cast-off from someone on the chain gang?"

"My coat?" said Joan. "No!"

"Well if I were you, little Joan, I would spend some time on my appearance. There's only so much mileage you can get out of pity."

"What do you mean, pity?" Joan had recovered to the point of feeling insulted. "Whose pity?"

"Whose do you think? You probably think you're hot stuff just because you managed to convince Dick you're worth his time, but where is he now? And how long do you think you'll hold his attention with that little girl act once he comes home a man?"

"This is still about Dick?" Joan asked, incredulous. "Gloria, Dick and I—"

"Don't be too sure of *anything* where you and he are concerned. Have you taken a good look at yourself? At least I'm improving myself."

"I'm improving. . . " Joan said, losing her train of thought. What had Gloria meant by the 'little girl act'?

"Oh are you?" Gloria harangued on. "How? By learning how to put shells together with glue? That ought to come in very handy when a man wants dinner."

By that time, Bernice had gotten close enough to hear, but stayed incognito, out of respect for her friend. The verbal beating she was taking was demeaning, but Bernice felt confident that Joan could handle herself, and eventually would come out on top.

"I am a very good cook," Joan argued, looking around to see if anyone was listening. "I've won contests."

"Oh good for you! But what do you *do*? Do you have a brain? I'm training in medicine. When the month is out, I will be certified. What will you be—oh, pardon me, besides a fixture in church all the time?"

"Yeah, you'll be certifiable, all right," Joan said, getting in a good punch.

"Huh! What good is all your praying going to do you? You are just wasting your time, you little fool. Dick has probably found a much better girlfriend by now. I don't see him anywhere, do you?" Gloria looked around exaggeratedly, waving her arms and flashing her perfect fingernails in Joan's face.

"For heaven's sakes," Joan nearly shouted. "There's a war on! He's not here. He's, he's. . .and I'm not his girlfriend. I'm his *fiancé!*"

But Gloria was not to be intimidated. "Oh *sure* you are," she shouted back. "I don't see a ring!"

Joan drew her hands into her pockets, suddenly aware of the raggedness of her coat, and a nick on one pocket. It was true. She did not wear his ring, but that meant nothing.

Gloria's voice had softened, and Joan thought maybe she had felt bad about what she had just said. She leaned toward her adversary just in time to hear her last words for that encounter.

"Let me tell you, goodie two shoes Joan Foster, praying all the time doesn't make you or Annie or any of your church buddies special and it's not going to make a lie into reality. You might as well face facts. You and your friends are dreaming if you think you can hold onto men. I heard Annie's fellow hasn't bothered to contact her in months, and where *is* Dick anyway? He hasn't contacted you either, has he? Face it, these men are simply *not* interested in the likes of you!" Her voice rose to a squeal at the end.

Something about Gloria's nerve, her fancy fingernails, Joan's former hopes for peace between them being crushed, and most of all, Gloria's repulsive suggestions about Annie and Sly created a jagged verbal razor blade of abuse flowing out of Joan's mouth.

"Well I think you are the one who is delusional," she began coolly, "because no couple is more dedicated than Annie and Sylvester, and too bad if that makes you envious. And I'm sorry you don't see the value of spending time in prayer, but don't you *ever* raise your voice disrespectfully against that again. And one more thing, Miss I-think-I'm-the-World, Dick Thimble has never, and I mean *never* had the slightest interest in the likes of you. Who would take the time to get to know a nasty-mouthed woman who can't seem to stand being in her own skin. Every opportunity you get, you berate people, you lie, you cheat, you would probably even steal from your own mother, if you haven't already!" Joan's voice rose. "When I think of you, I can't imagine what man would even give a half-hour of his time, with your false behavior and insincerity. Do you think we didn't notice how you tried to douse me again last month at the diner? Don't you love how it backfired on you? Well guess what, that's how everything is going to end up in your life, you nasty, red-headed street tart!"

Gloria was surprised by Joan's powerful response, but by the time she got to the end of her speech, Gloria was fired up again. How dare this pathetic threadbare urchin insult her that way!

She raised her big yarn bag to clobber Joan on the head. But just then a female, but rather muscular arm restrained her, pushing the bag up in the air, its contents falling out and scattering across the sidewalk.

"Oh no you don't," said Margaret, seeming to have appeared out of nowhere. "Joan can call you any flavor tart she wants. It's an unusual form of insult, but it's allowable. But there will be no violence."

"Oh yeah! And what gives you the right, you, you *gorilla*!" screamed the very frustrated Gloria.

"I'm with Civil Defense," Margaret said, pointing to the patch on her jacket. "I could have you arrested for attempted violence against a citizen. And I am not a gorilla. I am a primate, however, as are you."

Gloria shook her head, looking as if she were afraid she'd stepped into a lunatic asylum. "Who the hell are you?"

Margaret raised her hand again, "Public Ordnance 17 prohibits the use of public profanity. This is your last warning. I must urge you to desist and move along." As she spoke, she took Gloria's arm, and ushered her a few steps down the sidewalk.

Gloria pulled her arm sharply out of Margaret's grasp, straightened her clothing, replaced the items from her yarn bag that were flitting around in the wind, gave Joan one final sneer, and strutted down the sidewalk.

All the while Margaret spoke, Joan had stood motionless, having shocked not only Gloria, but herself as well. When Gloria retreated, Joan let loose the hot tears welled up within. It was then that Bernice approached them.

"How could I have said such things!" Joan cried.

"You were provoked," said Margaret. "It's natural you would react that way."

"Yeah, where were you?" Bernice asked Margaret. "I saw them, but I didn't see you until the very end."

"I have my ways," said Margaret. "I notice *you* didn't intervene. Aren't you supposed to be a friend?"

"I am a friend," Bernice said, "and I planned to intervene—"

"When?" demanded Margaret, "When Joan was wearing all of those contraptions out of that girl's bag for a hat?"

"Well, I didn't realize—"

"I did, and I was on the job," said Margaret.

"Thank you, Margaret," Joan said, getting a hold of herself.

"You are welcome. It's my job, and I do it well." She threw Bernice a superior look.

"You do. That's for sure," said Joan.

"Yes, I gotta give you that," Bernice said.

"No false praise, please," Margaret said to Bernice. "I have to move along now. Good-bye, Joan." As she continued down the sidewalk, she threw a look of disdain over her shoulder at Bernice.

"She still blames me for her breakup with the boy," Bernice said.

"I know," said Joan, mostly recovered. "What a morning. I thought this was going to be such a nice day."

"She had it coming, Joanie," Bernice said.

"I know, but I just hate losing control of myself," Joan said. "She won that argument because I really said some things I should not have."

"I think it was inevitable," Bernice said. "She's been on your case for over a year now."

"She's just hurt, wishing she had won out."

"That's for sure!"

"What did she mean about improving herself? That was surprising," Joan said.

"I think she's on the First Aid track, you know, replacing some of the folks that have had to go overseas," Bernice answered.

"That's a pretty good thing to do, I guess."

"Yeah. Even if her reasons are skewed."

"Well, skewed or not, I'm feeling pretty guilty."

As they walked along, Bernice elbowed her, "It might have been understandable, but you still gotta go to Confession."

Joan sighed. "I know."

"Why don't you go on home and get cleaned up. I'm sure Annie will be fine for a half hour or so."

"That's a good idea."

They walked a little further, then Bernice chuckled and said, "Geeze Joan, 'nasty red-headed street tart'?"

Joan covered her smile with her hand and shook her head.

Chapter Nineteen

Annie opened up the shop a little late that morning after going to the hardware store to see if they had any discarded boxes. Her beautiful statues were practically selling themselves, but she hated sending them out the door without secure packing. That meant a box with some kind of stuffing.

She'd found an assortment of boxes as well as old newspapers. Thanking the proprietor, she started on her way to the shop. With the bulky bundle obstructing her view, she almost missed a step down, but managed to recover. It was slow going from then on. The wind was rustling the papers and the packages, partially blinding her way, but eventually she got to her shop, entering through the side door.

I should have asked Joanie to come with me first thing, she thought. That was a four-eyes-on-duty kinda job. Boy, it was scary! She set down the boxes and turned on the light switch. The lights flickered, as they had been doing for days. She glanced at the fuse box behind the column of newly acquired boxes, wishing Uncle Paulie had taught her about electricity. Having someone come and look at that would not be cheap. The receipts this year were good, but not good enough to pay extra services, and even if they were, who could come? Every available electrician under 50 was overseas, she thought, and the rest are performing way more important jobs than seeing about a tiny little shop with flickering lights.

She busied herself inventorying what remained from her Christmas orders. She was very pleased with the success. When she came to a statue of St. Michael, she smiled, having an inkling that maybe Joan was going to see about that one today. Little did her friend know, but Annie had every intention of letting Joan have it at cost.

Why do I string her along? Annie wondered. She's been helping for weeks, and I can't just tell her right away? She wrapped the statue separately and set it in a box inside the glass case. That way, she reasoned, no one will see it and think it's for sale.

The wind blew hard and she felt the windows rattle against the walls.

"I'd better go and secure those a little better," she said out loud as she approached the aging walls. "You never know when we're going to get a blizzard this time of year."

About fifteen minutes later, she heard another puff of air. She shook her head, thinking to herself, I really need to get some tape or something for those windows.

With her face in the books, she began to reminisce about the summer barbecues in the Victory Garden at Helen's. How nice and warm it was then, she thought. Father and Monsignor were there, and what a wonderful—huh?

All at once, she was aware of smoke filling the air. It seemed to be coming from inside her shop somewhere. For that moment, all her mind could conjure was more German dangers—they'd started a fire in her shop. They'd somehow seen Joanie and her and they were taking revenge on Annie's shop because of the trouble she and Joanie had caused.

She grabbed a hold of the gallon pitcher of drinking water. The smoke seemed to be coming from the stack of boxes. Maybe they'd gotten at her by dropping something in one of them when she was walking to the shop. Afterall, with the boxes in her arms, her view had been badly impaired.

Without thinking anything further, she splashed the gallon of water right at the boxes, but it was futile. The smoke kept coming, and in fact, it looked thicker.

Could be it has nothing to do with the Germans, she decided. Scanning the room, she thought oh dear, some of those boxes might have contained chemicals, flammable things!

She approached the stack to see what was going on when one of them suddenly burst into flames. It was then that things really began to go badly for Annie. Instead of stepping back as would have been wise, she followed her curiosity, which took her even further into an already very dangerous situation. Her thought had been correct: inside several of the hardware store boxes remained flammable residue.

Seconds before she would have reached the stack, the fire hit the chemical residue, exploding the load of boxes with force enough to send Annie flying backwards. She was knocked unconscious when her head hit the display cabinets, leaving her body in a heap on top of an old carpet and some shop towels.

Quickly the flames ate through the boxes, lapping wildly into the nearby spaces, searching for something else to consume. Three and a half feet away stood the stack of newspapers, dried and perfectly seasoned for igniting. But the lack of oxygen in the tiny shop tamed the fire's appetite, buying time that would prove very fortuitous.

Smoke was rapidly replacing oxygen, putting Annie in great danger even if the fire could not reach her yet. But smoke was also blasting out the sides of the windows, sending unintended signals to anyone who happened to be alert to danger.

While Margaret's civil administrations regarding Gloria's attempted violence against Joan had slowed her down somewhat, Margaret had a remarkable ability to cover territory quickly. Due to her concerns about the sincerity of Gloria's agreement to cease and desist, Margaret had herded Gloria along ahead of her as she marched toward her job at St. Benedict's.

"You don't have the right to drag me to the church," Gloria objected as she skittered forward awkwardly.

"I have the responsibility to keep the peace," Margaret said. "You represent a threat. Your life-saving training is admirable, but starting fights is not allowed, and it's my duty to make sure that you cool off sufficiently."

Gloria secretly wondered if Margaret was some sort of superhuman. She had never experienced another female with such physical strength. "Well," she said.

Margaret nodded. The guilty rarely had anything to say for themselves, she thought.

It was then that she noticed the smoke coming out of the side of the church building. "That's the shop!" she said, "Annie's shop!"

And she took off at mega speed, dragging Gloria along who was too surprised and winded to object.

Seconds later, they arrived at the side door. Margaret grabbed Gloria's scarf to help her open the door, waved through the smoke, spotted Annie, and fireman-lifted her out the door all in the space of 10 seconds.

Once outside, she set her on the grass and checked to see if she was breathing. "Gloria, she's not breathing," Margaret said. "Make yourself useful and resuscitate her while I see if there's anyone else inside."

"I'm not breathing into her mouth!" Gloria protested. "That's disgusting."

"Oh yes you are, unless you want to go to prison," Margaret said, her glasses only an inch from Gloria's nose.

"Oh," Gloria said, "well, if she's not breathing, I guess I could try."

As Gloria took over, Margaret charged into the building and found that no one else was inside. She located the brand new 120-pound fire extinguisher, hoisted it on her shoulder and applied the chemicals from it to the fire. Fortunately, the flames had died down. Once she was sure the fire was out, she stomped on the boxes and pulled the power lever inside the fuse box, spotting the blackened metal and scorched electrical wiring.

Once outside, Margaret was pleased to see that while Gloria had departed, Annie was sitting against the grassy hill, breathing on her own, but unfortunately, covered in soot. Her face was so dark it looked like she was going night camouflaging. She was coughing hard and retching intermittently.

"Margaret," she started.

"Don't try to talk yet," Margaret said. "I was going to call the ambulance, but I see one has come. Are you hurt?"

"I'm not sure," Annie whispered, her voice hoarse. Then she began to cough harshly.

"Just wait for the medical personnel."

Annie reached for Margaret's hand. She couldn't hope to form any more words just then, but her eyes were filled with the most sincere thank you she had ever felt. However, as if that look had exhausted the last of Annie's strength, she immediately passed out, slumping backward against the grassy hill.

A short time later, Helen, Joan, and Bernice waited in the Emergency Room for news about Annie.

"Let's talk about something else for a while," Helen said wisely, watching Joan pace in the hospital waiting area.

"Easier said than done," said Bernice, tapping the table with a magazine she had tried to read.

"We don't have to stop thinking or caring, but talking might help us to get our feet on the ground," Helen said. "Remember, the doctors said she was breathing on her own, and that is a very good thing."

"Okay," Bernice said.

Joan nodded, but continued to pace, grasping and ungrasping her hands together. She could only repeat to herself the very first thought she had had when she'd gotten the news about Annie and the fire. *I should have been there!* If she had not stopped to spar with Gloria, an incident which had completely lost any significance to her, she would have been there to help Annie.

Alternatively, had she not stopped, she might have been another person to need rescuing, Bernice had reminded her. Which was true. Who's to say she would have played the heroic role that Margaret had. Margaret. Oh the times she'd sought to avoid confrontation with her, and now look what a miracle she was! Joan wanted to cry. Of the guilt and the shame, the shame was worse. Margaret was definitely peculiar, but that did not make her any less respectable. In fact, it was just one of her unusual characteristics—her seeming lack of emotion—that had made her so valuable in saving Annie's life. Annie's life. It seemed unbelievable that it had actually been at stake. Was at stake, still.

"She's not following orders," Bernice said in a low voice to Helen, indicating Joan. "She's feeling guilty that she wasn't there."

"Oh dear," said Helen. "But I guess that's natural. I feel a little of it myself."

"Well, I don't," said Bernice. "But I am glad Margaret was there."

"Gratitude, yes," said Helen. "That's most important. Maybe we should visit the chapel."

Joan turned her head and nodded hopefully.

The chapel was a beautiful, candle-lit arrangement of 14 split rows of pews and an altar with a Communion rail, divided in the center. A statue of St. Rita sat at the entrance on a graceful pedestal and one of Jesus, arms open and welcoming.

The three women remained in prayer while the hospital personnel carried out its duties, caring for the wants and needs of patients and patient families.

Down the hall, in the emergency room, Annie lay, receiving oxygen and being monitored by a kindly Sister. After a while, Sister stood to retrieve a book and began reading softly in case Annie could hear.

"'We are the three who come to save you,'" Sister read. "'That was quite a fall you took, but you seem to be a pretty tough young man,' said the fellow with the orange hat. 'But we'll have you fixed up in no time.' And the three set about bandaging the young man's head, and sewing his tattered clothes when all of the sudden there was a knock on the door.'"

And then there *was* a knock on the door.

"How is she doing, Sister?" the doctor asked.

"She's peaceful," Sister responded, smiling. "No twitching or anything. I think she'll be just fine after she comes out of the anesthesia."

"Good. Shame about the leg, though."

"That *is* a shame," Sister agreed. "But you certainly do beautiful work, Doctor."

In time, Helen, Joan, and Bernice returned to the waiting room and continued to wait for news, but with renewed spirits.

"Well I have something to say," Bernice said.

"Oh yeah?" Helen asked.

"I had a chance to talk to the attorney about the tax due."

"Mr. Wheeler, isn't it?" Joan asked.

"Yeah. I have some time to think about it, but I think I'm going to follow his advice. He feels that I could escape most of the incredible tax bill by donating certain buildings and then just selling others. Plus I can just keep things as I originally planned with the nuns' convent."

"That's good news," Helen said. "Does that take care of all of the tax burden?"

"No, but what more I need can come from the investment funds, I think he said."

"Well as long as you have them squared away, and the grocery is still yours, you're in good shape," Joan said intending to encourage her friend.

"That's the problem!" Bernice answered with surprising emotion. "I will have less to work with concerning that store, and I just honestly don't know what I'm doing. I really want to learn about it, but it confuses me."

"Do you mean the management?"

"Well, in a way. It's mainly the part of management that deals with figures and what to order and how much I'll need in profit to reinvest in the feeding people kind of program I'm doing."

"So basically you're saying it's the math, the accounting that's got you worried?" Helen asked

"Yeah. I've always been awful at figures," Bernice said sadly.

"I can understand that," Helen said nodding. "They've never been my strong suit, either. The best I can do is pay my bills without bouncing a check."

Joan stopped suddenly and pointed a finger in the air.

"Well I have great news!" she cried, startling her two friends and several people in the waiting room. "Sorry!" She stifled a giggle. "But I do," she continued softly. "Laureen's fiancé, who as you know is right here in the hospital, is an accountant! Maybe he can take it on."

Bernice and Helen looked at each other. Bernice was about to say something when the doctor appeared. All three girls were instantly on their feet, bracing, as if they were about to run a race to Annie's room.

He raised his hand. "No, no, please have a seat. Annie's mother asked me to give you a message."

"Annie's mother?" Joan asked.

"The family arrived about half hour ago. You must have been in the cafeteria," he said.

"Oh. No, the chapel, but please go on."

"She'd like you to know that Annie's thinking of you, and she's doing well, but we can't release her until tomorrow when we're sure she can manage her crutches."

"Crutches!"

"Yes, she's suffered a broken bone in her leg. It's a little bone, but she's in a cast and will be for about 6 weeks."

"Doctor, can we see her?" Helen asked.

"I'm afraid it's only family for today," the doctor answered, shaking his head.

"We're *like* family," Joan persisted.

"No, it's okay, come on, Joan," Bernice said. "We'll see her tomorrow, back at home."

"Yes, she should be able to go home tomorrow," the doctor said.

As the three of them stood to leave, Joan said, "Tell her we love her and we're praying for her, and that we'll come get her as soon as she calls."

"I will."

"Well that's a relief," Bernice said as they gathered their things to leave.

"It sure is!" Joan said. "But I wish we could see her."

Helen was about to agree when she spotted Monsignor Kuchesky. "Isn't that Monsignor? Maybe we can request a prayer for her?"

"Good idea, Helen!" said Joan, waving to him.

"Hello, hello ladies!" Monsignor greeted them. "I know why you are here. I heard about our friend, Annie."

"She's lucky to be okay," Helen said.

"She's a very special lady," Monsignor answered, "and a lucky one to have such devoted friends."

"We were going to see if you had time to—"

"Oh my yes," Monsignor interrupted her. "I will offer the Mass tomorrow for her rapid recovery." He paused to look warmly at Joan. "Dear Joan, I just want you to know that I am forever grateful for your discovery of the Lithuanian nativity set. It has given me such joy."

"I hardly did anything!" Joan answered. "But I'm glad it brought you some happiness."

"It has, but the news will bring even greater happiness to the Lithuanian royal family. From what I have learned, a chalice and ciborium were also brought to America in the hopes of protecting them. They were valuable of course, but they are precious to us all as having served as holders of the Eucharist and Precious Blood."

"What a shame that they weren't saved as well!" Helen said.

"I imagine it was the material value the thieves were after," Bernice said. "Were they solid gold?"

The Monsignor nodded. "Yes, but after all, they were only metals, huh? What is more Sacred than the life Our Lord has given us? And today, Annie has held onto hers!" He smiled sincerely, casting a warm feeling instantly over the group.

"Amen to that," said Helen.

"Yes."

"Are you seeing patients today?" Bernice asked.

"Yes, indeed. There are quite a few, so I'd best say farewell. I will give your love to Annie when I stop in to say hello once they have moved her to a room."

"What a good man," Helen said as they continued toward the parking lot. "Bernice, I can't thank you enough for driving. I know it will cut into your gas ration, but it was certainly a big help not waiting for the next bus."

"Oh don't mention it."

Joan cleared her throat.

Bernice stopped walking. "What?" she said.

Joan giggled. "I was actually just clearing my throat," she said. "But I did want to ask you two something. Earlier, I was having, let's say a discussion with Gloria."

"I'll say!" said Bernice.

"What's this?" Helen asked, giving both girls the once over.

"I'll tell you about the rest of it later," Joan promised. "But one of the things that really seemed to bother Gloria is our praying."

"Our *praying?*"

"Yes, she mentioned it two or three times, that we think we're holy, that I should have been a nun, a lot of things. It made me wonder, do you think we're, or I at least, am too showy? Or make a display out of it?"

Helen shook her head. "I've been told the same thing. And usually by someone who is wishing they spent a little more time in prayer. Joan, there will *always* be detractors. Sadly, it's human nature. And ironically, it's *more* prayer that helps us stay strong and maybe ushers some of that bitterness from out of their hearts."

"Very well put," said Bernice. "I agree one hundred percent. In my bit of experience, it's usually someone who's unhappy who strikes out at a person so fundamentally."

Joan nodded. "More prayer," was all she said.

Two floors up inside the hospital, Bob McGarrett lay, physically better, but tortured by the words he had said to Laureen. His appetite had declined. As he lay there, staring at the wall, his nurse, Sister Veronica Ann, tapped him on the shoulder.

"Feeling poorly?" she asked.

Bob nodded.

"Shall I get the doctor?" Sister asked with a twinkle in her eye, knowing the answer to the question.

"No, no," Bob said. "It's not that kind of badly."

They sat in silence for a while.

"Sister," he said at length, "may I request a visit with Father Bertrand?"

Sister Veronica Ann smiled. "Of course."

The diRosa family was not an altogether quiet one. Their expressions of love and relief coupled with gratitude and even scolding could be heard well down the hall.

From her bed in the middle of everything, Annie listened, her leg propped up on two pillows, an enormous plate of food in front of her. Mama finished issuing warnings and turned to Papa to scold him about not having his brother make sure the shop was in tip top shape for Annie. For heaven's sakes, what do girls know about electricity? Why would he leave her in such a mess?

Papa's argument was well, maybe Paulie didn't know it was damaged, and maybe even it *wasn't* when he left. It's been a couple of years now, maybe it just got that way.

Mama returned her attention to Annie, stroking her hair, speaking lovingly in Italian, as her father turned away to hide a tear.

Just outside the door, a figure stood, attempting to be nonchalant, but in fact, listening earnestly.

"You are a treasure," Annie's mother said.

"Oh ma," Annie responded.

The figure outside the door involuntarily inhaled sharply, surprising herself with her degree of emotion. She looked around hoping no one had noticed. Sisters were passing, carrying trays and pushing carts, but none of them seemed to have noticed.

"Don't you never get mixed up in any kinda fire again, you hear, Pica?" Papa said.

"No, Pop, I'll be more careful," she said, but shrugging to her mother behind her father's back.

Her mother punched her on the shoulder. "He means it," she said.

"You bet I mean," her father said, his voice rising. "Aint no fire gonna take away my only daughter!"

"You can't control everything, Coro," her mother said.

As the discussion rose in volume again, Annie's roommates began to shift uncomfortably in their beds. Sister appeared in the doorway, her finger to her lips.

"It's time for our patients to be sleeping soon," she said. "We'd best keep our discussions at a low level, *sta bene?*"

Annie's mother smiled at the effort at Italian, and nodded. She and her husband began gathering their things together as a neighbor and his son, and one of the bakers at the shop who had come along to wish Annie well, filed out of the room.

"Thanks Ma," said Annie. "I'm going to be okay. The girls'll come get me tomorrow."

"You sure? I can take off of work," her mother said.

"No, no, Bernice has got a car. We'll be okay. Thanks for all the goodies. Ti amo."

"Anchío ti amo." I love you, too.

The redheaded figure outside the door quickly withdrew, her expensive heels clacking down the hall in a hasty retreat. She grabbed a hanky from her purse and dabbed at her eyes, smoothed her red curls, and ducked into a waiting car at the entrance to the hospital.

As it pulled away, Gloria Marini sat silently in the back seat, mourning the love of family she had never known.

Chapter Twenty

At Helen's house, the next morning, despite the cheerful prognosis of their friend, the atmosphere was dismal.

"This close to Christmas," Joan said, straightening the tablecloth. "It's so hard to believe such an abysmal thing actually happened to Annie!"

"I wonder how she'll do on crutches," Bernice said. "I've never tried them, but every time I see anyone using them, it looks like they're about to faint."

"I once *did* see a girl faint, right in church," Joan said. "But I think she must have hit herself in the head or something."

Despite the heavy mood, Helen could not help chuckling. "I'm thinking yes, getting clobbered on the head might cause someone to faint."

Helen's reaction tickled Joan. "I think I might have expressed that wrong," she said, laughing. "She really did though, gave herself a good whack on the noggin with the wooden handle. Down she went."

"Ouch," said Bernice.

"Well," Helen mused, "I guess we should be happy that we'll be bringing Annie home today and that she's only in the hospital overnight. It could have been a lot worse, you know!"

Joan nodded. "Yeah, I don't even want to think about what *could* have happened."

"I wonder what kind of shape the shop is in," Bernice said. "Thank God that Margaret was able to put out the fire so quickly."

"Oh that reminds me," Helen said. "Margaret stopped by very early and announced that she is opening the shop! Apparently she contacted Annie's mother at the bakery and offered. Her mother was happy for her to do it. It was very thoughtful of her. These next couple of days will be the busiest of the whole season for vespers shopping."

"That's for sure. I think I'll give her a hand. Margaret is really a very good friend, isn't she?" Joan said softly.

"Yes, she is, to all of us," Helen said. "I get choked up thinking what might have happened if she hadn't been. . . patrolling."

"Yes," Bernice said nodding slowly. "She is, for all of her oddness, a good and caring person. And think about the presence of mind she must have had to be able to find the fire extinguisher, put out the flames, and then just kind of fearlessly stomp out the smoldering boxes. It really was heroic."

Joan wiped away a tear, shaking her head. "She saved her life, didn't she?"

Helen nodded. "She's not the kind that wants a lot of fanfare. In fact, she made that very clear on the phone. But I expect the two of them will share a special bond after this."

"I'm sure they will!" said Bernice.

Joan felt a twinge of something just then. She couldn't define it, but it wasn't pleasant, and she didn't want to prolong it. She nodded and smiled.

Just then, the tea kettle began to make noises, hovering near the screaming stage. Helen got up quickly, intent on preventing it.

"More tea anyone? I'm having some."

"Yes, thanks," said Bernice.

After another round of tea and still no phone call, Joan was getting worried. "You don't think anything happened overnight, do you? Like maybe she got worse or had a relapse?"

"In order to have a relapse, you have to be sick to begin with," Bernice said. "All she did was break her leg."

"All she did! How would you like to break your leg?"

"I don't mean it's not serious," Bernice explained gently. "I just mean you can't relapse from a broken bone. It's either broken or it's not. It doesn't break again over night."

"And don't forget, she breathed in a ton of smoke!" Joan argued, as if she hadn't heard anything Bernice said.

"Girls, don't get excited," Helen said. "I'm sure she's fine. You know how hospitals are. They are probably having trouble locating her is all."

"Trouble locating her!"

Bernice grimaced at Helen.

"Yes, she's probably going from bed to bed in the men's ward, getting names and phone numbers for possible dates for Margaret!" Helen laughed, drawing the others into it, as they imagined the scene.

"I can just see it!"

"She's probably filled up a couple of notebooks by now!"

Just then the phone rang.

Helen got up. "Keep your fingers crossed!" she said.

Moments later she returned full of cheer. "Okay girls, time to go!"

The hospital parking lot was fuller than it had been the previous evening, so it took much longer to get to Annie's room.

There was Christmas music playing from somewhere, and Annie was fully dressed, sitting on her bed with her leg raised on two pillows. "I was about to give up on yous guys!" she said as they piled into the room. But she instantly reached out for hugs and was bombarded with them.

"Oh thank God you're all right!" Helen said, sniffling.

"Hey Joanie, move over," Bernice said. "I want a hug, too!"

"Get your own Annie," Joan said in a muffled voice, but merrily.

"Get in here, Bern," Annie said grabbing her. "Just don't sit down on my leg."

"Does it hurt?" Joan asked, drawing back to look at Annie's cast. "Gosh, that's a big one!"

"It surprised me, too," Annie said. "They told me it was only a crack and that it was in a little bone, but then they stuck this giant thing on it."

"Whatever they did, I'm sure it's because they feel you need it," Helen said. "They're just being thorough. And with this mob, you're going to need all the protection you can get."

Annie smiled. "Thanks guys, really," she said. "It's been lonely here without yous. We always say we're going to stick together, and when we can't, it's really hard! We're indivisible." Her voice cracked when she said *indivisible*.

"We woulda visited," Bernice said, "but it was just family last night. In fact, Joanie put up her dukes and she was getting ready for a fight."

Joan laughed. "Yeah, and Helen was going to call her contacts here and see if we could bust you out during the disturbance I caused."

"But I was the calm one," Bernice said, "and my cooler head prevailed."

"Your cooler head, my—"

"Ask her about Margaret," Helen intervened, raising her eyebrows at Joan.

"I was only going to say *eye*," Joan protested.

"Okay. But I want to know, what Annie's been up to since last night. I see a wheelchair here."

"Yep," said Annie. "I have a very friendly nurse, Sister Ann Bernadette. And she let me go and see the guys, as long as I didn't overdo it. I told her I wanted to thank them, and she really liked that idea."

"Wow, so you went into the men's wards?" Joan asked.

"I sure did. Sister said she does it, why can't I? And she wheeled me through. We didn't see the seriously injured or the burn victims, but there are so many, Joanie. You wouldn't believe it. They are wards, like lined up beds in a nursery or something. One right after the other."

"Bob's room was different," Helen said, "but I'm guessing that's because of the special care he and his roommate both needed."

"Yeah," Annie agreed. "I only saw the mobile guys. They had been serious and were getting close to release or they were here overnight for something. Really nice men."

"Hobnobbing, huh?" Bernice asked. "Anything Sylvester should know?"

"Sylvester," Annie said. "I had such beautiful dreams about him. Can you believe it's been almost a year?"

A silence fell over the four of them as they remembered the previous Christmas, each relishing her own memories. Who could have imagined back then that a year could pass and still they were without their loved ones?

Annie shook it off. "Well, I didn't waste all of my time. We went around again this morning, and I think I might have found a prospect!" Her eyes glittered.

"A prospect!" Joan said, appalled. "Annie!"

"Not for *me*, silly, for Margaret."

Just then a Sister entered the room. "Looks like you're all checked out," she said, smiling. "Now remember to keep that leg elevated, and by all means stay off of it." She turned to survey Annie's companions. "You look to be in pretty good hands," she said, winking at Helen.

"I can go now?" Annie said, sounding very young all of the sudden.

"Yes, ma'am. Here, let's get you into this wheelchair and we'll wheel you down and as far as the car. After that, these ladies will help you into the house so that you don't become tempted to put any weight on that leg."

As Joan helped Annie turn around and into the wheelchair, Bernice glanced out to see if the way was clear. She thought she caught sight of a familiar redhead. In a flash, she was up and around the corner, peering down the hall. Sure enough, about twenty feet away, hurried Gloria Marini, her telltale heels clacking out their familiar attitude against the shiny tile floor.

I wonder what she's doing here, Bernice thought. Obviously she's not injured. I never gave a thought to whether she had close family.

"Hey, what are you doing out there?" Annie called from her room. "Mine sweeping?"

"Yeah you never know," Bernice said.

"With hundreds of service fellows in here, I think we can rest assured she's safe," Helen said, pushing Annie's chair through the doorway.

Joan carried her things, which included four packages of goodies from her parents and neighbors. "These look good," she said smiling, raising her eyebrows.

Annie giggled. "That one's for Margaret," she said, pointing to a brightly wrapped box.

Joan studied the box as she walked.

Bernice followed along, occasionally looking back to see if Gloria had returned to the scene.

After a very slow but careful journey back to Helen's house, Bernice pulled into the driveway and shut off the engine.

"Are you gonna make us walk from here?" Annie asked. "Not that I'm complaining or nothin'"

Helen opened the door and reached for Annie's hand. "No, I asked Bernice to bring everyone here. I think it would be nice for us to have a little slumber party for the next few days. We have Christmas Eve and Christmas, and Annie, getting you in and out of your house so many times, I don't know."

"A big slumber party!" Joan said, "what a great idea!"

After Annie was inside, leg properly elevated, and Helen in the kitchen getting something for everyone to nibble on, Bernice drove Joan back to their house to pack some clothes.

"I feel like a celebrity," Joan said, "getting driven just around the block!"

"This wind is fierce today," Bernice said. "We can't risk getting sick now with Annie incapacitated so close to Christmas."

Joan shook her head as they entered her house. "What kind of Christmas will it be?" she said. "Bern, it's so hard to bear up under this unknowing. It's like walking in the dark sometimes."

"I know."

"It's awful what happened to Henry, and Bob, too," Joan went on. "But at least we know. It's so hard to just know *nothing!*" Then she turned and looked at Bernice. "I'll stop. I can be such a baby sometimes."

"You're not a baby, and you're right. My relationship with Henry isn't like yours with Dick, but you can believe I had some dark nights wondering what might be happening to him. His mother didn't hear anything for months, you know. Then all the sudden, there he was, in that English hospital."

Joan grabbed her arm suddenly.

"I know it's not much comfort," Bernice said.

"No! It's a lot of comfort," Joan said urgently. "Did you say his mother hadn't heard from him in months?"

"Oh yeah, from I think the spring, May or something. Then in November, there he is!"

"No Bernice, that gives me so much hope! And you've got to tell Annie. I don't think she knows about that either."

"Geeze, I never even thought about telling anyone—it didn't seem like anything."

"That's okay!" Joan said, her eyes shining for the first time in weeks. "It's probably the best Christmas gift I could ever get."

Later that night, as Joan snuggled into the cozy blankets of one of the twin beds in Helen's guest room, she felt peaceful. "Annie," she whispered.

"It's lights out," Annie whispered back, giggling.

"Lights out!" Joan said out loud. "Who says?"

"Shh! I think everybody's asleep!" Annie whispered.

"No we're not," said Bernice from the sofa.

"This is so nice," Joan said. "I never went to college. But I bet this is what dorm life was like. All of us girls together."

"I don't know, I didn't go either," said Annie.

"Me either," Bernice said, "but I bet you're right."

"Last time I spent the night out was in Atlantic City, for that wonderful dance you gave me your ticket for, Annie," Joan said. "That changed my whole life."

"Yeah," said Annie. "You stayed with Margaret."

"Margaret, yeah, and Laureen was there. I have to get in touch with her. It's been days."

"I really hope Bob comes around," Bernice said. "She must be really going through it."

They lay in silence, pondering Laureen and Bob's tenuous situation.

After a while, Annie said, "It's hard to sleep with your leg up in the air."

That made everyone laugh.

"I'm serious. You try it! It ain't fun!"

"No thanks," said Joan. "We're going to need all our strength to cart you around all day."

"I knew I shoulda gone on a diet," Annie said.

"Yeah," said Bernice, "talk about wearing out your welcome!"

"Well if it's too much—"

"Only kidding!" said Bernice. "Right Joanie?"

"Yes, of course! Although from what I hear, Margaret's the one with the muscle."

"Yeah, Annie. Did you know she picked you up, slung you over her back and carried you outside?"

"No," Annie said softly. "I knew somebody did, but I didn't know it was her. She didn't tell anybody."

"Well I saw it!" Bernice said. "And she ordered— hey, did you know Gloria gave you mouth-to-mouth?"

"Ew!" said Joan.

"No! It was that or, you know, curtains," said Bernice.

"Wasn't she breathing?" Joan asked.

"I don't know, but Margaret gave her the order, so she must have thought she wasn't."

"Well, she might have been breathing, but she wasn't thinking," Joan giggled. "Imagine trying to put out a fire with a half a gallon of drinking water!"

"She? You mean me, right?" Annie said. "I didn't die. I'm still here."

"Oh don't worry, we can hear you!" Bernice said.

"I can hear *all* of you!" Helen called from her room, startling them. "Go to sleep! It's late!"

Joan and Annie giggled. Just then the clock chimed midnight.

"Did you know it was that late?" Joan whispered.

"No!" Annie whispered back. "Oh, and by the way, I did get a date for Margaret!"

"No kidding! Nice guy?"

"Yeah, he seemed really nice and looks like her type. You know, kind of stalwart and independent."

"Good looking?"

"Pretty good looking. He's a sergeant."

"Hey! We all have sergeants then!"

Annie and Joan giggled again.

"Go to sleep!" Helen called.

Chapter Twenty-One

Bernice pushed open the kitchen door to Henry's house, as had become the routine. Knocking made little sense. Besides, Bernice thought smiling, he's got to be running out of smart responses to my tapping on the door.

She stepped inside, and checked the note tacked to the wall near the kitchen sink, just inside. *Appt. 11:30 am with Dr. Mitchell*, it said. She had known about it and saved her gas ration specifically for that purpose. Her little coupe didn't take much gasoline to go a mile, and fortunately, it was only a few miles to the hospital. She found herself wishing again that government had planned better when it came to gasoline rations for the servicemen. Those with medical discharges were just about the only ones home, but they had no better allowances than housewives. How were they supposed to make it to and from the hospitals?

Well, no matter. At least for today, everything was fine. She tapped on Henry's door and looked in. "Doing okay today?" she asked.

Henry was sitting up and was mostly dressed already. "Very well," he said smiling. "I think I'm ready for the test. They will find me to be healing perfectly."

"Good," Bernice said nodding. "We have a couple minutes. Do you want to go about this gradually or just wait until it's time to go?" She sat down at the edge of his bed.

"Go about what?" Henry asked, reaching for a glass on the table.

"Oh let me get that for you!" Bernice said, jumping to her feet.

When she handed him the glass, he took it with what seemed like a bit of a jerk. "Go about what?" Henry repeated, his voice a little clipped.

The sound of his voice reminded Bernice of a time years before, when Henry had been denied the chance to do something he wanted to do. Inside she smiled, amused at the thought, but outwardly, she was on guard. "Getting dressed," was all she said.

"*We* don't need to go about it," Henry said. "I'm doing just fine."

"Good," Bernice said. "Well I'll be in the kitchen if you need me." As she left, she felt a pang of pride at his defiant attitude.

His pride seemed to carry Henry quite a way, but by the time he got from his bed, through the door, and to the car, his pride along with his body, were about tuckered out. He stood by the door, summoning the strength to open it. Bernice stood behind him and to the right. She didn't say a word.

Henry ducked his head down and up a few times, as if he were pumping the sink in an old-fashioned kitchen. He started forward smoothly and latched onto the door handle. But that was as far as he could manage. He turned his head slightly to the right, a sheepish smile on his face.

"Yes?" said Bernice, stifling a laugh.

"Okay, maybe I do need a little help," Henry said quietly.

"Well, if you think I'm going to lift you over the threshold. . ." Bernice giggled.

Henry smiled. "Maybe just open the door and give me a little push."

Bernice helped him into the seat. It was a wide, bench-type seat, very comfortable once one got in. But the challenge was getting up over the edge to sit. She heard him gasp a couple of times, which made her cringe, but she kept quiet.

Once they were on the way, Henry said, "That old guy in London, Bern, he would not have needed someone to get him into the car. He was amazing, after all he'd been through."

"Did somebody blow out his guts with a machine gun?"

"Rifle," corrected Henry. "No." After a while, he started up again. "But he went through plenty—I don't even know the half of it—and twice!"

"Listen Henry," Bernice said softly as she turned onto 23rd Street. "That old man was a gift to you, an inspiration. He brought you around in a really tough and bitter time. But I doubt he would have thought less of himself if he had needed help. Surely he didn't find shame in it. He would have been gracious, maybe even laughed at himself, the way you describe him."

Henry nodded. "That's exactly how he would have been," he agreed. "I'm sorry, Bern. I'm trying to make things just as they were, and they're not."

Bernice's heart ached for Henry, sitting there trying so desperately to be strong and independent. She knew if she showed sympathy or pity, it would serve only to further his doubts. After a few moments, she tapped the wheel and nodded. "It's just going to take time, like the nuns told me. So many things these days, the only medicine is time."

Henry nodded. "You're right," he said. "Your driving's a little jerky, but you're right."

Bernice smiled. "Yeah? And who taught me, Professor?"

"Oh yeah."

At the hospital, Henry was taken right away to his appointment, so after a bit of waiting, Bernice decided to catch up on her morning prayers, which she had neglected in favor of taking Henry that morning. But as she entered the long hallway, she spotted the familiar figures of Father Bertrand and Monsignor Kuchesky.

"Bernice St. Claire!" Monsignor boomed, startling the nurse on duty. "How nice to see you!"

"Good morning, Monsignor. Good morning, Father," she answered. "What a surprise to see you! Although I guess you make visits here a lot."

"We do," said Father Bertrand, "although we seldom see each other when we do. We were just saying what a coincidence to have completed our work at the same time on the same day."

"What brings you hear?" Monsignor asked. "It can't be the weather."

Bernice giggled. "No, but actually I don't mind the cold weather so much once it sets in."

"It sets into my bones," said Monsignor. "That's the part I don't like."

"Let's sit down," said Father Bertrand.

There was a small waiting area nearby.

"To answer your question," said Bernice, taking a seat, "I'm actually escorting a wounded serviceman."

"Oh my!" said Monsignor. "That's a great service."

"Well, he happens to be a friend," Bernice said smiling.

"Henry?" Father Bertrand asked.

"Yes," Bernice answered. "It's his first appointment since he arrived home from England. I think he might have been a little nervous, but if spunk is any judge of health, he's got nothing to worry about."

"That's good," Father Bertrand said, nodding. "Henry's a good man. He's lucky to have your friendship."

"I knew a young man named Henry," Monsignor said. "He was quite a character. All fire and wild at first, but in time he settled down."

"Was he. . . rescued, too?" Father asked.

"Oh my no! He was in the hospital with me," Monsignor said. "He was terribly wounded. But like your friend, he had that inner strength. I think you called it 'spunk.'"

They were all nodding happily when suddenly Monsignor looked as if he'd been struck.

"Is it your heart?" Father Bertrand asked, jumping to his feet. "Shall I get the doctor?"

But even as he spoke, the Monsignor's face broke into a broad smile. His tearing eyes were focused across the room. Bernice and Father turned to see Henry standing there with an equally shocked expression on his face.

For a second no one spoke, then suddenly both men moved forward as rapidly as their battered bodies permitted and met halfway with a warm and lasting embrace.

Bernice and Father Bertrand exchanged confused glances.

"You wanna let us in on the mystery?" Bernice asked.

Father Bertrand chuckled.

Henry and Monsignor parted then but sat immediately next to each other. Henry shook his head. "How?" was all he could manage.

Monsignor chuckled and looked at Father. "This is the man!" he laughed. He turned to Henry. "It sounds silly, but we were just talking about you! Just this moment!"

"So this is the man you knew?" Bernice said to Henry.

"Yes! This is that very holy man I told you about!"

"How long have you been here," Monsignor asked. "I came last summer."

"Only a little while. I still had some patching up that needed doing after you had been discharged," Henry said.

"What a blessed meeting," said Father. "You'll be happy to hear that Monsignor Kuchesky will be here with us for quite a while."

Henry smiled and shook his head. "That's *everyone's* blessing," he said.

Father rose. "I will take this opportunity to meet with someone who has requested a visit," he said. "Please, take all the time you like."

"Yes," said Bernice. "I can take care of some things, too. And after you get caught up, we'll have to plan one of Helen's marvelous get togethers."

"You know Helen?" Monsignor was asking Henry as Bernice headed for the chapel.

Her heart was filled with the excitement of the moment and gratitude for prayers answered. She didn't know how God would handle it, but she'd prayed for strength for her friend. There it was, in the form of the beloved and robust man who had such depth of understanding and love for people. Even better, he understood what only men such as he and Henry *could* understand.

She hadn't realized it, but in the commotion, she had shed a few tears which had begun to roll down her nose. She grabbed a handkerchief to wipe them away and stuffed it back into her pocketbook.

"Did something happen to Annie?" asked a familiar voice.

She looked over her shoulder to see Gloria Marini hunched over, as if sharing a secret. She was not quite herself, Bernice noticed. Her usually beautiful outfit and hair both looked somewhat disheveled, as if she had slept in her clothes. Her eyes seemed a little wanting and maybe more recessed. Maybe she hasn't slept, thought Bernice, or perhaps hasn't seen the inside of her makeup case recently.

"What are you doing here?" Bernice asked. What was going on? Had she suddenly stepped into a novel by Charles Dickens?

"Answer me! Did something bad happen to Annie?" Gloria repeated, her eyebrows drawing together angrily.

"No, nothing bad happened to Annie," Bernice said.

"Well, I see you crying, and she's not in that room anymore. Did she have to have surgery or something?"

"Annie's home," Bernice said. And cutting to the chase, "What do you care?"

"I *don't* care," Gloria said, adjusting her jacket.

Bernice noticed that the sleeve was scuffed and a little soiled. "What are you, shoveling coal these days?" she said before she took time to think.

Gloria looked stunned. "What a thing to say!"

"I'm sorry, I just noticed that you are not, let's say, your usual impeccable self. Your sleeves, for instance—"

"Are *none* of your business!" Gloria shot back. "Who are you? The Style Enforcer?"

Bernice held up a hand. "Okay," she said, and continued on toward the chapel.

"No!" Gloria called. "Stop! Wait." She teetered forward on the hard, tiled floor to catch up with

Bernice. "I, I'm, well, anyway. I was just concerned, that's all."

Bernice tried to hide her incredulity, but she failed. "You're concerned? About Annie?"

"Well, I *did* help revive her," Gloria said, a distasteful expression crossing her face. "I'd like to know how. . . well, how it all turned out, I guess."

"Oh."

"Well, how did it?"

"She's fine. I mean she has a broken leg, but she's fine."

"Nothing serious or more serious, then."

Bernice had begun to grasp that Gloria had had some sort of epiphany. She immediately felt ashamed that she had assumed the worst and felt the need to extend an olive branch. "It's really very kind of you to be concerned," she said. "I guess I didn't expect that."

"Well." Gloria fiddled with her earring for a moment. "You girls, the four of you, seem to be so, well, close or something. Always hanging around each other."

Bernice felt hopelessly dense. What would one say to that remark?

"You have real friendship," Gloria went on. "You seem to be there when one of you struggles or, you know."

"Yeah," said Bernice.

"I guess I just wonder how to achieve that."

"You mean friendship and caring with other people?"

"More like having people around when you need
them."

Bernice was moved. How could she have
misjudged this poor girl for so long? Maybe Gloria did
some catty things, but apparently, inside, she longed
for the same friends and closeness that everyone else
needed. What a beautiful revelation. I should invite her
with me to chapel, she decided. We can share a
moment of peace and then maybe have a cup of coffee
together.

Smiling broadly, Bernice opened her heart to Gloria.
"Would you like to come with me? I'm just heading to
the chapel to say some prayers for friends and the
servicemen, you know."

But abruptly, Gloria shrank back repugnantly, as if
hit in the face with a pie. "*What?* Pray? Are you crazy?"
she shrieked, turned, smoothed out her hair and
proudly clacked down the hall.

As Bernice pondered her visit from the funny farm,
Father Bertrand tapped lightly on the door to Bob
McGarrett's room.

"Anyone home?" he asked lightly.

"Oh, hello Father," Bob said. He was sitting up,
working on a crossword puzzle. "Thanks for coming."
His manner was polite but forced.

"This is turning out to be quite a day," Father said,
pulling the chair nearer to Bob. "We just found out that
one of our hometown boys and our visiting resident
Monsignor were real close buddies overseas. They
never expected to see each other again, but today they

came across each other right here in the same town! Do you know Henry Harper?"

"Henry. . ." Bob mused a moment. "No, but I think I heard the name mentioned."

"He's friends with Bernice and the girls," Father Bertrand went on casually. He noticed Bob's demeanor beginning to relax. "He was gravely injured in Italy. Spent a long time in an English hospital but since he's been back, things seem to be looking up. He was able to get to an appointment today, and to his great surprise and joy, meet up with Monsignor."

"That's quite a coincidence!" Bob said.

"Yes. Both of them were somewhat overcome by it, I think. I've left them down the hall to talk. I thought it might be a good time for us to visit. You know, just talk, if that's all right with you."

"I appreciate that Father. Everyone says you're the man to talk to about these things."

"I don't have all the answers," Father said thoughtfully, "but through the years, I've seen a lot of young men find their way back. War seems to affect each person differently. There's no proper procedure, no course of treatment like these folks have here in the hospital."

"I'm happy to hear you say that," Bob said. "I've been wondering how it is that a lot of these guys just come through and they're absolutely fine except for their physical injuries."

"Hey, don't believe that for a minute," said Father. "In some ways, it's better when the soldier struggles at first. Some of the emotional wounds hide out for a while and then when they make themselves known, they're that much more difficult to overcome."

"Well, I don't see how anyone could fail to feel the guilt over what I've done."

"Son, in war all soldiers are put in the position of having to kill—"

"No, it's not that. I knew that when I joined. I understand that. It was kill or be killed. That isn't what's ripping me up inside."

"Go on," said Father.

"My squad leader, Master Sergeant Dick Thimble. You know how you talked about Henry and the Monsignor, that friendship? It was even more with me and Dick. We knew each other before the Army. And then we went through Stateside assignments together before we both got immediately shipped out. They saw his leadership qualities right away and he skipped right up to Master Sergeant."

"Must be quite a guy," Father said.

"He is. Or was. Or is. That's where this black blanket of guilt comes, Father. It's eating me alive. He was fine—we were all kidding him about his wound. And he was laughing. We all got hit, and I was worse, least I thought so. Next thing I know, something's wrong and he's down. I mean really badly. I know I told you all this before. But I still know nothing. They sent him on to the States, and I prayed and prayed when they got me here that he'd be okay."

"What have you learned since you arrived?" Father asked gently.

"I didn't find anything! He never got here! I been here for weeks now, and still there's no sign of him. What does that tell you? If he left ahead of me and he's not here—maybe he's not coming, maybe he didn't make it." Bob had worked himself up to the same desperate level of guilt and frustration that he had suffered daily. He slumped over Father's arm, clinging to his shoulder and sobbed.

Father remained quiet, letting Bob release the energy that had tortured him for so long. He took out his handkerchief, to have it ready, and simply waited.

Finally Bob sighed heavily and raised his tear streaked face. Father handed him the handkerchief and put a steadying hand on his shoulder.

"Sorry to be so emotional," Bob said.

"It's an emotional issue," Father said with understanding. "I'm glad you've given yourself a little relief."

"It does feel that way," Bob said, "like some relief."

They sat in silence for a while. Bob leaned back against the wall and sighed heavily. "The pain is not just losing a trusted friend, but not knowing what happened to him. Where. . ."

"When a man I know spoke to me about this very situation some years back," Father said, "I told him what someone had once told me, years before that. We want to know these things, it's natural. But trying to work out the answer isn't something you can do with a pencil and paper; you can't scroll through your mind and pinpoint an answer. You have to sit back and accept that in time, it will all be clear. Bob, you've done nothing wrong. There's no room for guilt. You've been severely wounded defending along with your brothers in arms and are healing well. I believe there are people in your life who care for you. You seem like a reasonably healthy person, so you must have family and friends. Be with them. Share your life and all of what God has allowed you to keep. Through that appreciation of life, you will find happiness.

"And the reality is, you don't know about Sergeant Thimble. I happen to be well-acquainted with his fiancé. She has no doubt whatsoever that she will be in his arms again one day."

Bob lightened up. "You know Joanie?"

"Yes, very well."

"We introduced them to each other."

"We?"

"Laureen . . .oh, Laureen," Bob trailed off, remembering their last meeting.

"Is that your young lady?" Father asked smiling.

"Yes, well, she *was*."

"Well then she's one of the wonderful gifts in your life."

"Yes, she is a wonderful gift. But Father, I've been awful to her." Bob's face began to grow dark again.

To his surprise, Father Bertrand stood up quickly just then, and very lightly said, "Well, nothing you can't make right again."

"But this is serious," Bob insisted. "I mean, I'm not sure, but we might have even broken up."

"Well if you can't remember. . ."

"No—I think she said, or I said. I don't know who said it, but our visit didn't end well. Father, I've got to talk to her!"

"Well, maybe I can convince her to give you another try," Father said with a twinkle in his eye.

Bob smiled and nodded. He was exhausted. "Thank you, Father. For everything. Thank you. Please do that."

Father backed out of the room smiling. "I plan to," he said.

Much later, Helen, Bernice, and Joan, with Annie sitting on the couch, began to set the table for supper.

"It's a wonder you girls are still awake after staying up half the night giggling," Helen said, smoothing out the tablecloth. "My iron was acting up. You can sure tell it on this corner."

"I am sleepy," said Annie. "But I think it's because I sit around all day doing nothing."

"Probably," said Joan.

"Yeah, you lazy nag," said Bernice.

Annie stuck her tongue out.

"When Laureen gets here, she's going to have to help us clear and wash up while you sit over there and watch," Joan teased.

"You know I'm glad Laureen's coming," said Bernice. "I saw Father at the hospital today and he had a favor to ask you regarding Laureen."

"You saw Father?"

"I have a lot to tell you guys, in fact," Bernice said nodding. "But first, Helen, do you want the blue and white dishes for tonight?"

"No, better use the floral," Helen said, retrieving the dinner plates from the hutch. "I've got leftovers on one of the blue and whites and I don't think we'll have enough of them. What's the favor?"

"Yeah, Bern, what's the favor?" Annie called, beginning to feel left out.

"Well it's *my* favor," said Joan.

"Yeah, it's yours, should you choose to accept."

"What?"

"It's like this," said Bernice. "Father wants me to ask you to ask Laureen if she'll give Bob another chance."

"Father? What, did he see Bob today?"

"I guess so."

Bernice proceeded to update the girls on the happy meeting between Henry and Monsignor Kuchesky, finishing with, "And I've been trying to figure out all afternoon how to relate a strange conversation I had without it being gossip. I don't think it is gossip because it's more strange than anything else."

"Strange conversation with Father Bertrand? Geeze Bernice, you better watch what you say," Annie said.

"No, with Gloria Marini."

"Gloria?" said Annie.

All the girls stopped what they were doing and turned to look at Bernice.

"Yes, Gloria." Bernice looked at Annie. "About *you!*"

"Me?" Annie said, looking around the room. "I thought her beef was with Joanie, no offense."

"Huh!" said Joan.

"She caught me by surprise, accused me of crying about something having happened to you," Bernice said.

"You were crying?" Helen asked.

"Well, I must have been, but I didn't realize it, you know, during the whole reunion with Henry and Monsignor."

"Oh," said Helen nodding.

"I assured her that you were fine, except you had a broken leg."

"Yeah, I'm fine," said Annie. "Just a broken leg." She shook her head.

Joan giggled.

"All right, you know what I mean, smarty pants. So after a while of talking with her, I realized she was wanting friendship, you know, closeness with people."

"*Gloria?*" asked Joan.

"I know it sounds funny, but she kind of let her guard down and said she noticed we four were always together, doing things together, caring about each other. She said it as if she wanted the same for herself."

"My stars," said Helen.

"So what did you say?" Annie asked.

"That's just it. I thought well, maybe she wants to be friends. It's hard to make friends sometimes, and she might be the type who seemed mean but was actually just shy. I thought it might be a good opportunity to talk and maybe she'd like to come pray with me and then have a cup of coffee. When I suggested she come with me to the chapel, you might have thought I asked her to kiss a horse. She was positively incensed and stomped off down the hall."

"You thought she'd come to chapel?" Annie asked.

"I know it sounds unrealistic," Bernice said. "But the way she was talking, I was sure she'd had some kind of breakthrough."

"Well. . ." said Joan, shaking her head. "I don't know. I can't imagine that myself. And after her reaction to your suggestion, I kind of doubt that."

"Gloria Marini, hmm," said Helen.

Bernice scrunched up her face, seemingly staring at the utensils in her hand. "I don't know. I could swear there was something, but I could be wrong."

"It's very good of you to give her the benefit of the doubt. In fact, this might be a signal for us to be extra charitable toward her," Helen said. "You never know what is in a person's heart."

Just then, someone knocked on the door.

"It's Gloria!" called Annie from the couch and covered her head with the blanket.

Helen shook her head and Joan giggled.

Joan opened the door to find Laureen. "Hi there! We're just setting the table, come on in."

Laureen's normally lustrous golden hair was pinned back and, along with her eyes, seemed to have lost its luster. Joan took her coat and admired her outfit. She wore a plaid pinafore and bright white blouse with black tights and black flats. "Hello everyone!" she said.

Her voice was hearty enough, but to Joan it had the sound of one pretending hard to act happier than she was. "Let me have your coat," Joan said. "You look so pretty!"

"Thanks! Smells mighty good in here!"

Annie pulled her head out of the covers. "You're in for a treat, Laureen," she said.

Laureen gasped. "What happened to you?"

"Oh nothing happened, really," she said looking at Bernice. "Just a broken leg."

Joan giggled.

"Well I'm glad you don't let it get you down," Laureen said laughing.

"Yeah, she won't let it get her down, but she'll milk it for all the sympathy she can get," Bernice said.

"Come in and sit down, Laureen," Helen said. "These girls have a long-running joke about Annie's terrible accident. We'll tell you all about it at dinner."

Helen brought out two delicious casseroles. One was all vegetables mixed with a cheese and milk sauce accented with savory spices and topped with crunchy potatoes. The second was a chicken and noodle dish with parsley and paprika that Bernice could not get enough of.

The dinner conversation was happy and hopeful, in bright contrast to earlier nights.

"I'm so glad we decided to bunk together," Helen said after dinner. "I think it's just the thing we needed."

"I love it," said Annie. "I wish this is how it always was."

"I don't know whether Sylvester would agree with that," Laureen said, smiling. "It might be a little crowded for the menfolk."

The girls giggled.

"We've got some good fellows," Helen said.

"Well, some of us have," Laureen said, looking down at her plate.

Bernice elbowed Joan. "Your assignment, should you choose to take it?" she said under her breath.

"I know, I know!" said Joan.

Everyone waited expectantly, looking at Laureen, and then back to Joan.

"Am I missing something?" Laureen said. "What assignment is she talking about, Joan?"

"Oh, it's just a simple thing," Joan said. "I guess I just wanted to say you know Father Bertrand and all. He's such a fine priest and so inspirational. Don't you think?"

Laureen looked confused. "Yes," she said slowly.

"Well, he's always got ideas about how people need to be generous with each other—their hearts and minds, that kind of generous. And when, well, when we suffer rough times with each other, we should maybe take a minute to step back and look at things. The big picture, you know.

"The big picture," said Laureen, growing more confused.

"Looking at the big picture gives us a perspective on things, helps us to remember what's important versus what's only fleeting," Joan said.

"Oh for heaven's sakes!" said Bernice.

Helen chuckled, but said, "Leave her alone, Bernice, she's doing fine."

"If she ever gets there," said Annie.

Laureen had begun to smile by then. "What are you trying to say, Joan?"

"Well," Joan said, "Father made a visit today with a patient, and he got another portion of the picture."

"What patient was that?" Laureen asked.

"Well, Bob."

Laureen gasped.

"He believes that Bob is now, well, perhaps also capable of focusing on the broader picture of reality and, well the long and short of it—"

"Short, *please*!" said Annie.

"The long *and* short of it," Joan continued, scowling at Annie, "is that Father wanted me to ask you, if Bob asks you to visit, would you go? Because Bob wants to see you."

As if being directed by a bouncing ball, all four sets of eyes then traveled over to Laureen.

Laureen did not make them wait. And she didn't disappoint, either. "There's no other answer," she said, shaking her head. "Of course I'll go. Tomorrow morning."

Joan hugged her and the others applauded.

Laureen sighed. "Gosh, this is a nice place to be," she said.

"Be careful," Bernice shot out, "Joanie might be getting ready for another one of her long speeches."

"Well I liked it," Helen said. "Well done, Joan."

Joan nodded and made a face at Bernice.

Annie, whose leg had been propped onto one chair while she sat sideways at the table on another chair, had started to become uncomfortable. "Help me over there to the couch?" she said to Helen.

"Sure, honey."

After Helen had gotten her settled, she realized the day had gone so rapidly that she'd never been out to check the mail. She stepped out for a moment as the girls began to clear the table. When she came back in, Helen was holding a US Government letter.

Everyone froze.

"It could be anything, Helen," Annie said. "We've been through this before."

"Yeah, Helen. She's right," Joan said as Bernice moved in to get a closer look.

"Just open it, get it over with," Bernice said.

"That's exactly what I intend to do," said Helen. As she opened it, she steadied her hands by gripping the envelope tightly. "Oh!" she exclaimed.

"What?" everyone cried at the same time.

"Paper cut," she said.

"Oh."

As she read, Helen nodded some, and then closed her eyes and released a long sigh.

The others held their breath, eyes wide.

"Harry's rotation is up," she said, eyes still closed but smiling. "As soon as he is replaced, he is to be shipped home. For good."

The room exploded with cheers, tears, and congratulations. For the ladies at 6 North Edison that night, it might as well have been Christmas.

Chapter Twenty-Two

The weeks spent with the Italian farmer and his wife, after having been shot, of course, were nearly blissful for Sylvester. He thought of Annie as much as he wanted to without fear of weakening his battle resolve. Aside from the moments of great discomfort when it came time for changing his bandage, or those first few moments each time he moved into standing position, he was in no pain. To top it off, the farmer's wife was not only a nurse, but highly gifted in the kitchen, preparing dishes that returned Sly and Bobbie to health in rapid order.

It was a snowy morning in late December when the farmer and Bobby, who had recovered enough to walk a little outside, entered the kitchen where Sly sat eating breakfast. They were very excited.

"Yo Sly, how 'bout this?" Bobby said.

The farmer and his wife looked at each in confusion.

"Italian, Bobby," said Sly. "It ain't polite to talk English when they can't understand us."

"Sorry, yeah right," Bobby said. "Scusa. Abbiamo grandi notizie!"

"Come va?"

The farmer took over, smiling as he approached Sylvester. "Gli Alleati hanno sgomberato la foresta," he said. "C'è un percorso per le barche di salvataggio ora. You a, you a get a rescue!"

"No kidding?" Sly said. "You know what that means, Bobby? We're going home!"

"Entrambi!" Bobby said. "Both of us, and alive!"

As they were packing their things, Sly sighed. "You know, the papers we got said the rescue would take us to England, not home."

Bobby nodded. "Yeah, there's a lotta guys there. But them Army Medical folks was just going by old orders."

Old orders. Sly felt sad for the first time in days. It had been a lonely moment when the news of Harry's having been discharged reached them. "Harry gone—I can't believe it."

Bobby snorted. "Well, he ain't dead!"

Sly chuckled and went on with his packing. "I just thought, you know, like last year, maybe we'd all head home together, see the gals, our families."

"I know what you mean, man."

"All the things we been through together."

"Yeah, the great times—him and the guys starving to death, sitting in the rain for three weeks, oh and that great time I had dying from bad water. I see what you mean."

"Shut up," Sly laughed.

"It's funny, I seen it, too. The friendship, whatever you call it, friendship don't seem like a good enough word. It comes together before you know it's there." Bobby exhaled heavily. "Where do you figure they sent him, anyway?"

"Harry? I don't know. He's like a cat. Guy's got 9 lives plus! I hope they didn't send him closer in, that's all. He's in his fifties, for crying out loud."

"I thought he turned sixty."

"Mighta, I don't know. But wherever he is, I hope he's wearing his St. Christopher medal."

"Oh you can bet on that!"

Just then Batista entered, smiling, holding a cloth sack. "Eat. We have a eat a for you a trip."

The men stopped and thanked him. A lunch packed by Batista's wife would be heaven on the long journey out. His wife had gone to her room to cry in private, the farmer explained. She preferred not to say good-bye. His son had returned to the army by then, so it was only Batista to bid farewell.

Bobby and Sly shook hands with the man who had rescued them. "I'm so indebted to you, sono così in debito con te," Sly said.

"Ah!" Batista snorted. "Thanks to my son! Grazie a mio figlio!"

They all laughed, easing the tension.

"You're the best, Batista, sei il migliore," Bobby said, his voice breaking. "Grazie tanto."

Their hike was a necessarily and blessedly short one, as Sly was still heavily dependent on his home-made crutch, and Bobby's kidneys, which had been damaged, were still poorly and in need of medical attention. At the appointed junction, all went well, and within two hours, Sly and Bobby left the Army jeep and climbed into the transport vessel, and out in the deep water, boarded the ship bound for England. They thought.

Weeks earlier, the day before he had dispatched Sly on the mission to get Bobby to safety, Harry had learned that his orders to return to the US had come through. He had read over the page several times, his mind needing to be sure of the facts before he could believe it. That day, after his replacement had arrived, and he'd dispensed with all the good-byes, he'd taken up quarters on the ocean liner that would transport him first to Europe and ultimately to the New York Port of Debarkation.

It was a bittersweet prize to be going home. On the one hand, he wanted nothing more than to be in the loving arms of his wife, in her kitchen, enjoying her sense of humor and wonderful cooking. He no longer yearned for the adventure that had gotten him out there in the first place. Harry was pretty sure he'd had his fill.

Yet, the boys—all of them, really, but most especially Sly and Bobby had become like sons to him. Bobby was such a character, with his constant preoccupation with food, and his strictly Philadelphia way of saying things. When he last saw Bobby, the young man was not looking well. Harry hated to ponder it, but the reality was that Bobby may not have survived. The statistics he saw every week more than brought home the message how many men were lost due to ignorance of their surroundings, outside weather conditions, and traffic. The enemy was literally everywhere. The news of casualties and deaths was always dispatched late, so if Bobby had died, he probably would not know about it until he arrived home.

Sly was a horse of a different color, calm and restrained, careful about every word, probably would make a good diplomat Harry thought, laughing slightly. And he was a strong kid, probably northern Italian blood if I've learned anything from this war, he thought. Those men—all of the Italians, for that matter—in those regions seemed to be made of a very special kind of stock. They were not easily rattled. They could act, they could sing a song and convince an outsider that they were merely an innocent shopkeeper or waitress, but inside, boy, watch out. Fierce defenders of their towns, their homes, their people. That was Sly. And yet the man had a heart that seemed to beat only for that one girl, Annie diRosa. Harry hoped and prayed that that union would take place after all this. Some of the guys, he knew, would struggle after the war. But he had faith in Sly. That's one fellow who will plough through it all to greener pastures.

The ship was sailing smoothly through the Mediterranean, where it would pass through Gibraltar, now that Tangiers had been subdued, and into the Atlantic for the English ports of debarkation. Just before supper, Harry went above board to see the escorts and feel the sea air on his face. On the way, he came upon the scene of a wounded soldier, probably going home for good. At least, he thought, he survived, which was much more than so many others.

The soldier and his buddy stood looking out at the sea, their outlines silhouetted against the dusky grey sky. Harry felt a wave of emotion. He turned away to give them time alone with their thoughts and headed for the chow line.

After several days of dinner in the enlisted men's mess, Sly was missing the farmer's wife, more specifically, her cooking. "We been spoiled."

"You got that right," Bobby said. "Thank God it's smooth sailing so far. I don't think I could take a rough ride these days."

"You're doing pretty good," Sly said. "Tell you the truth, I wasn't sure how the waves would strike you."

"I think we dock pretty soon. Maybe my luck will hold out."

"I hope so. I wonder what they plan to do with me when we get there," Sly said.

"Teach you to dance with one leg?"

"Oh man, don't kid around like that. Let's change the subject."

"If you was that bad, Sly, they ain't gonna send you 'cross the ocean without a medical."

"I got a medical."

"Yeah, so do I. That just means we go to the hospital, right?"

"I don't know. I just got on where we're supposed to and follow the doctor's orders. He's a good guy."

"Yeah, I like him. No nonsense. I guess they'll tell us what to do when we get to the English hospital."

"Yeah."

They lay on their bunks, Bobby reading a magazine and Sly staring at one without really reading it.

Bobby kicked at the underside of Sly's bed lightly. "So did you get an allowance when you were a kid?"

"An allowance? Yeah. It wasn't much. Pop wasn't what you'd call liberal that way, but we got a you know, a few cents for the candy store."

"Yeah, me, too. Them was fun times, huh?"

"You know, I used to get kidded by my friends. I wouldn't spend it all, you know? I'd spend a penny, get maybe a penny's worth of licorice or some'n, and then pocket the two cents leftover. Put it in my bank."

"No foolin'!" said Bobby laughing. "What were you, the original Rockefeller?"

Sly laughed, and rolled over to get off the top bunk. He pinned his good leg on the edge of the lower bunk while lowering the other one down slowly. He bent his knee, and then popped down to the floor on the good leg. "Not bad," he said, complimenting his technique.

But just to be safe, he took a seat at the little table. "Yep, I got teased about that all the time. They called me 'Moneybags Bapini.'"

"I could believe it. You still got it, too, right?" Bobby asked, chuckling.

When Sly didn't answer, Bobby gave him an inquisitive look.

"What?" said Sly.

"You still have it? That money you got from your pop when you were a kid?" Bobby asked.

"Well, I got some of it, yeah. . .you know. I mean I don't think a man needs to spend everything he makes," Sly answered defensively.

Bobby walked up and down in the small cabin, shaking his head, amused but incredulous. Finally he stopped and turned to Sly. "Let me ask you something, Sly. When you open up your wallet, and you take out a couple bills, do the Presidents squint in the light?"

Just then the funny blast that the men onboard had come to recognize as a signal for upcoming announcements sounded.

"Assemble on deck in 5 minutes," called the announcer, who went on to state which deck and who was exempt.

"What do you think that's all about?" Sly asked.

"I don't know," Bobby said, "but I'll go. I'm faster."

The officers on board had met previously to determine procedures. Many of them were debarking in England, while others were going on to other ports. As they returned to quarters, the noncoms were called to receive instructions.

Bobby rushed by one officer about to enter his cabin, knocking into him slightly, saluted and apologized in the dim light and continued on. The officer paused, watched eyebrows raised as the young man hurried down the way, shook his head, smiled, and went inside.

Above, Bobby learned that those with medical papers were to wait to be transported until all others had departed, except for the crew of course. They were to receive information from the officer in charge of their cases.

When he explained that to Sly, the two of them tried to figure out if they'd be going to the same hospital.

"You got a leg wound and all, and them guys back in It'ly said it's gonna maybe need surgery," Bobby said. "That means a hospital for sure. Me, I don't know."

"Hopefully all you need is medicine," Sly said. "That's what the doc thought, remember?"

"Yeah, but he said he wasn't sure. They got new procedures, new stuff. I don't know."

"I guess we find out! When do we make England?"

"Tomorrow 0800."

The next morning, both men were ready well before docking at the port. The ship had seen absolutely no enemy attack, as far as they knew, and as they'd reached English waters, the crew and all those above board had given up a cheer.

Even with all the activity though, the Navy was strict, and procedures were going according to schedule. Bobby and Sly had the opportunity to watch the crews removing various cargo.

"Reminds me a little of Bari," Sly said.

"Yeah, without the explosion," Bobby snickered.

"Hopefully."

By 0815, they were called and assigned to their new quarters. "Actually," the officer stated, "you'll keep the same one. I trust it's comfortable for you," he said, smiling. "You are Ashenbach's men, aren't you? Okay, good."

Bobby opened his mouth to say something, but then looked at Sly. Sly looked down to study the papers, but the dispatcher quickly signed them, handed each a copy, and signaled for the next soldier.

"Um," said Bobby as the next man approached.

"Move along, soldier," said the officer. "We've got a schedule to keep. Return to quarters."

Bobby and Sly, both equipped with heavy duffel bags, moved aside, more confused than even before.

"So we're going back to Italy then?" said Sly.

"I don't know," said Bobby. "How long is the ship docking?"

"You're asking me? You better ask somebody who knows what the hell is going on." Sly said, irritated.

Returning to their cabin, they decided to unpack as they tried to understand what was going on.

"I don't even know who to ask. That officer said we were Ashenbach's men, which we are, but how in the world did he know that?"

"It must be on our orders. He's our CO, or was."

Sly sighed. "Maybe the medical was a medical leave—but we didn't really have leave."

"They don't have a you know, like a small treatment area on the ship or something, do you think?"

"No. If they did, we would have been getting treatment or whatever they were going to do to us during the last 5 days."

"Well I don't think I'm going to be much use to Harry in this condition if he's reassigned to another port in Italy," Sly said. "But in a way, we were in the Comm division. We weren't actually supposed to be in combat. Maybe they figure we're okay for linguistics, like we started out."

"That makes sense, except they don't have any way to treat kidney problems, least that's what I heard. On top a that, Harry might not be there no more, remember?"

The hoots and exclamations of the English soldiers disembarking were resounding in the halls. It cast an aura of depression over the two men, who had so recently thought they were about to step on friendly soil.

Sly flung the unpacked remains of his rucksack in a corner and slouched into a chair with a scowl. "Criminy," he said.

It was then that the funny knock came at the door.

"Now what?" said Bobby.

"Wait a second," Sly said to Bobby. "Did you hear that?"

"Yeah, somebody knocked on the door."

"No," said Sly. "Somebody *funny* knocked on the door!"

"Harry!" Bobby called out as he opened the door.

Harry stood in the doorway, grinning and shaking his head. "Don't I rate a hello, soldiers?" he asked.

Instantly the three old friends embraced like long-lost brothers.

"Come on in here! How'd you end up on this tub, Cap?" asked Sly. "We heard you went somewhere else."

"No, my Orders came through. I'm done, fellas. I'm going with you, straight through to debarkation at Philly."

Sly looked at Bobby. Bobby stood there, his brain working but no words coming out his mouth.

Sly recovered first. "We got leave?" he asked. "Again?"

"Philadelphia? *Philadelphia?*" Bobby repeated.

Harry chuckled. "Hey, let me ask you guys something. Did you look at your papers?"

"Yeah, we were just reading them," said Sly. "We're supposed to go for Medical treatment. But then dispatch up there told us to come back here, so we figured we were headed back to Italy, get medical treatment there maybe."

"Medical *discharge*," Harry said. "Discharge."

"Oh," said Bobby blankly.

"You're going home."

"Home? *Home!*"

"Both of us?"

"All of us."

"Home!" said Sly, finally finding his voice. "We're going home! Bobby, we're going home!"

Chapter Twenty-Three

Laureen was thinking about the parking lot, or the shiny floor under her feet, or anything but Bob. As long as she didn't dwell on it, she told herself, she could stay even, unflappable, the way she used to be.

But as she reached the room where she had last seen Bob, her heart began to thump, even jump a bit unevenly. She took a deep breath, held it, then let it out. She had discovered that doing that simple thing would help her steady herself. Joan had told her about it, and to Laureen's surprise, it worked instantly.

Laureen was carefully dressed for the occasion, a fresh blue dress with white lace around the skirt pockets and sleeves, and a ring of wider lace along the neckline. Her navy blue heels went together with it perfectly. If she had put more thought into it, she might have worn flats that were less attractive perhaps, but also less noisy.

The result was that by the time she'd reached Bob's room, he was on alert, sitting up, and waiting for her, thus spoiling her plans for a casual greeting, catching him off guard.

"Laureen! You came!" Bob said, grabbing his crutches.

His eyes were full of the love Laureen had longed for for such a long time, and all of her plans for a careful review of their last conversation went out the window. "Bob!" she cried, awkwardly but with great urgency, maneuvering around the medical bed and metal stool that separated them.

Their approach may not have been cinema worthy, but their embrace certainly was.

"I was so mixed up," Bob gasped between kisses.

"So was I," Laureen responded. "I didn't understand."

"I didn't understand either," Bob said.

The two of them stood together like a gothic statue with clothes until a nurse entered the room, stopped short, then continued, saying, "I *think* I have the right room."

Bob and Laureen withdrew, embarrassed.

"Here, sit down," said Bob. "Have a chair here."

"I only need to take a blood pressure reading," Sister said. "After that, he's all yours."

Laureen took a seat, smiling self-consciously, looking down at the floor.

Sister was finished in a flash. "You're in great shape, Sgt. McGarrett," she said. "It won't be long before we see you as an outpatient."

Laureen's eyes lit up. Sister exited the room, but then popped her head back in the door and said, "And I want this door to stay open."

Bob smiled sheepishly, and said, "Yes, Sister." He turned carefully and sat on the bed near Laureen and took her hand. "Only the highest respect."

Laureen felt a sense of deep, sweet peace that traveled through her body, giving her a chill. She shivered a little.

"Oh, I know it's cold in here," Bob said reaching for a blanket. "This one's clean, put this around your shoulders."

"I'm okay," Laureen said, but she took the blanket. "This seems like a really nice place. And you seem so much better, Bob." She smiled, shyly looking him in the eye.

"I am. In all ways," he said. "Once I got down, I just couldn't seem to get out of it, and I just kept making things worse. It was really your visit, honey, that helped me see things."

"And Father Bertrand, maybe?"

"Yes, and then Father Bertrand. Honey, he was really just reinforcing and telling me for sure what I figured was happening. You have no idea how grateful I am that you well, waited, or stuck around, or stood by me, however they say it."

"There's no one but you, Bob. I won't say I wasn't upset. But I guess deep down, I knew I just should have been patient, like everyone told me."

Bob smiled. "Everyone told you? Since when does that have any bearing?"

Laureen leaned against him. "Let's walk a little. Can you use those things?"

"My crutches? Oh yeah, I'm coming along fine." He struggled to stand, and one of the crutches went out from under him and he plopped back down on the bed. "See what I mean?" he asked.

Laureen giggled. "Let me help you."

"Okay with me," he said.

As they made it to the end of the hall, they turned the corner toward the intake gates to the patient loading zone, where new patients were wheeled in.

Without exception, each one was on a rolling bed, regardless of whether or not he could walk. As Bob explained about it to Laureen, he caught sight of a Douglas C-47 Skytrain. As the large plane finished dispatching patients from its giant belly, the ramp was raised, doors bolted, and slowly it moved toward the fueling depot.

Bob had no way of knowing that it had transported its patients from an Oklahoma Hospital. Nevertheless the sight of it made him feel melancholy for that moment, yearning for old times.

Yet, as he began to sink into that familiar malaise, Father's words revisited and he remembered to leave all things in the hands of the Almighty.

Laureen was not oblivious to his quick change, but she waited for him to speak. She didn't know what the big plane meant to Bob, and while she longed to understand, she knew Bob needed his own time to manage it all before he could share it with her.

Bob squeezed her hand, grabbed hold of his crutch and they moved slowly toward the intake doors. Several stretchers were being pushed through a set of double doors perpendicular to their hallway, and a couple of others sat waiting.

One of the stretchers was occupied by a clearly impatient soldier. He sat up, his back to them, swinging his feet to and fro in some kind of rhythm. He wore a heavy cast on his left arm, and a very rough looking blanket across his lap. Laureen leaned toward Bob and giggled. Bob smiled. But then something got his attention, and he squinted hard at the soldier.

"Nah," he said, softly. But at that point, he turned toward Laureen and said, "I guess I'm not as strong as

I thought. Would it be okay if I took a little nap? I think they might be letting me out of this place tomorrow."

"Oh of course!" Laureen exclaimed. "I don't want to wear you out. Tomorrow's Christmas Eve, you know."

Their eyes met, Bob's even more filled with joy than before. "I know it!" he said. "Christmas Eve!"

Laureen felt his sudden surge of joy, accepting it with gratitude albeit with a little confusion. Maybe he's grateful that he's ready to go home, she thought as they returned to his room. Seeing those soldiers just coming in probably made him realize it. Then a thought occurred to her. "Where will you stay?" she asked.

"Father's invited me to stay with them until I'm better," he said.

"Oh no you won't!" Laureen shot back, startling him. "You'll stay with us. Mother said so."

Bob laughed heartily. "Well, if *mother* said so. . ."

Down the hall, the orderlies had returned to roll the next set of patients in, but seeing the one sitting up, the old orderly took a moment to study his chart.

"Ah, you're here for discharge, huh?" he said. "Done your time, hey Sergeant?"

The soldier could hardly contain himself. "I believe that's how they phrased it. All right if I take a stroll around the place?"

"Long as you don't go far. Says here you got kin? You know where you're staying?"

"Not yet," said the soldier, hopping off the gurney and padding down the hallway in his socks.

As soon as Laureen had left, Bob got back up and grabbed his crutches. That blanket on that soldier had his optimism soaring. His mind cast back to the days in Oklahoma before he and Dick had shipped out. That blanket, or its identical twin (a thought Bob would not permit himself to consider), would lie neatly across the end of Dick Thimble's bed every morning on top of sheets as tight as a drum.

"Where'd you get that old thing?" Bob had asked him one day.

"What this?" Dick said. "That's my old Pawnee blanket. I had that thing since I was 8 years old. Might have left it, but you know, it's my good luck. Keeps me warm, and I like it."

Bob remembered the preceding summer, which had seemed like years before, how he'd hoped to meet up with Dick before he got evacuated, but he'd looked for him, and sadly just missed him. He hoped that Dick had just been moved for tests, but when he saw that the blanket was gone, he knew Dick had been taken.

But then today. His breath raced through his body as he raised himself up on his crutches. He worked them smoothly, gliding through the door and down the hall, thinking it wouldn't be long before he'd be an expert. But when he turned the corner and looked down the hall, both the gurneys and soldiers were gone.

"Darn!" he called out, loudly enough that he saw two Sisters' heads pop out in opposite directions from rooms on the hall. Their expressions started out sternly but both then turned amused, as they returned to their patients inside.

Well what's so darn funny? Bob wondered. He shook his head and pounded a crutch on the floor. He must have been dreaming, he decided.

But just as he started to move again, a very familiar voice, although slightly fainter, simply said, "Behind you."

Bob turned around, lost his balance and would have fallen to the floor if it weren't for the one strong arm of Sergeant Dick Thimble. "I gotcha!" he called.

Upright again, Bob and Dick stared at each other, unsure what to do about the waves of completely unfamiliar emotion rolling through them. Finally Bob grabbed his buddy in a bear hug, as he balanced on his good leg, letting the crutches drop. Dick hugged his friend with his good arm, balancing the two of them on his two good feet.

After a moment, Bob stood back. "Where the hell you been?" he cried.

At that point several nuns' heads popped out, one of them sternly shooshing him.

"I'm sorry, Sister," said Bob. And to Dick, whispered, "Where the hell have you been?"

Dick burst out laughing. "Come on, Crip," he said giving Bob the support of his good arm, "I'll tell you all about it."

Still a ways out at sea, but getting closer, Harry, Bobby, and Sly sat talking about everything that had happened since they had seen each other last.

"It's good they sent you two home," Harry said. "I don't know how much longer your luck would have held out."

Sly shifted his leg. "I guess we were lucky at that," he said.

"Yeah," said Bobby. "We didn't die. That's all Debbie said was, hey Bobby, she goes, I don't care how you come home, just not in a box."

Sly chuckled. "She really say that?"

"Well, not those words, I guess. But I got her drift."

"You might just make it," Harry said, tapping on a cigar. "These things don't wanna stay lit."

"You like a cigar?" Bobby asked.

"Not really," said Harry. "Just some'n to do."

Bobby laughed.

"Helen don't care if you smoke," Sly said.

"Helen," said Harry. He looked away for a moment. "Guys, I can't believe I can finally see her again, and our kitchen, and my chair. It's gonna be something."

"Me, too. Eatin' at the diner," Bobby said. "Can't wait!"

Sly and Harry laughed.

"Every time I think about Annie, I gotta stop," said Sly. "I just worry it ain't true, that maybe something'll happen and I have to drift away again."

"I know what you mean," Harry said. "In fact, you know, everybody has a little of that. You will be happy to be back, and you'll be glad you're not going out again. But believe it or not, there's an adjustment you gotta make. I'm telling the truth. It's not easy being back."

Bobby and Sly looked at each other.

"Nah," said Bobby.

"Yeah, Harry, I don't think I'm going to have to worry about that," Sly said.

"We never had no trouble before," said Bobby. "It ain't like we're going to a new city or something. We're going *home*. Geeze, I hope we are anyway!"

Harry chuckled. "Okay, I know how you feel. But do me a favor guys. I been through a war before and sometimes problems come up, things you can't believe or don't expect. How about we stick together, stand up for each other. You know, we'll hang in there if one of us has a problem."

"Like a pact?"

"Yeah!" said Sly. "Okay, count me in, Cap."

"Me, too," said Bobby. "All for one and one for all."

Chapter Twenty-Four

Helen had arranged her three, red star poinsettias in the center of the dining room table, each wrapped in foil and red crepe paper. She had dipped cranberries in a honey glaze and set them in the pots on toothpicks as edible decoration. With Annie's bakery goods coming, her table would be a welcome sight for company.

Helen's kitchen was always a cheery affair, but on Christmas Eve, it was a treasured memory in the making. Cheerful giggling filled the room, as Joan, Annie, Bernice, and Helen butted and elbowed each other repeatedly, while seeking enough space to mix up, roll, or cut out their special Christmas treats.

"I'm glad we all started out right here in this house today," said Bernice. "It's about zero degrees out there! I wouldn't cherish trying to walk through this weather! Look at those icicles, Helen!"

"I know it," said Helen. "I'm going to have to get out there with the hoe or a shovel or something and bat them down."

"Oh let them stay," Joan said. "They're beautiful and they're not hurting anything."

Annie hobbled over to the window and looked out. "No, Joanie, if somebody walked under one of them and it fell, they'd be really injured."

"That's for sure," said Helen. "I've even heard of deaths caused by some bigger than those."

Joan shivered. "I had no idea. So you've got your own weapons cache, huh Helen?"

"Let me see what you're working on, Joan," Helen said, approaching her side of the kitchen. "Oh aren't those darling! I love Christmas trees!"

"I like the way she's decorated them," Annie said. "Joan, you will forever be the most creative person I know."

Joan smiled. "No, I think that accolade belongs to you, Annie," she said.

Bernice shook her head, looking down at her cookie sheet of decorated dough. "You know girls, this is one thing I don't think I'm ever going to get the hang of. Do any of you know what these are supposed to be?"

Annie shook her head. "Hmm, are they scrolls, with little lines of verse on them?"

Bernice stared at her and said flatly, "No."

"Let me take a look," said Joan, setting down her shaker of green sugar. "Oh, she said, thinking as hard as she could. "Sure, those are," she turned to Helen who had begun to study the dough blobs on Bernice's tray, "elves? Santa's helpers. Aren't they, Bernice?"

Bernice tilted her head to the side. "Elves?" she said. "No."

Helen wasn't about to make a guess after the other two had tried and failed. After all, as kind as they wanted to be, Bernice's figures did not really look like anything, except maybe blobs of raw dough. It was probably in the transfer from the rolling board to the tray when they'd lost their shape. "Well I can't see what you've got," Helen said, "but I betcha they taste great. Is Henry coming tomorrow?"

Joan and Annie exchanged glances which seemed to say, "That Helen can do anything!"

"He and his mom, both, for a little while," Bernice said.

"It's so nice to hear that he's getting so much stronger," Helen said.

"I think it's amazing. He had a very serious injury. But he says they had really good care at that hospital in England. The nuns were amazing."

"I know another good little nurse," said Annie with a twinkle.

"Me, too," said Joan. "Bernice, you are the real healing touch for that man. I think you two have a really strong bond."

Bernice paused, spatula in hand, looking at the ceiling. "We really do," she said. "I was worried that it might be uncomfortable between us, but it's really been anything but that. I sometimes get the feeling that Henry might also be called."

"Called?" said Annie, turning to Bernice.

"I hadn't heard," said Joan. "Do you mean he wants to be a priest?"

"Wouldn't that be wonderful!" said Helen.

"It's not as if he said anything directly," Bernice answered. "But he understands what I'm thinking about and how important it is to me to share that life with the Sisters. Sometimes I get a feeling that he's about to say he's considering the same thing."

"That would just be terrific," said Helen. "How was his visit in the hospital yesterday. You never got a chance to tell us about it."

"He's really progressing well," Bernice answered. "The doctor said there's no reason he can't be fully independent within weeks."

"I'll bet he was happy to hear that!" Annie said. "He won't have to ask Auntie Bernice to go to the bathroom."

Bernice gave her a shove with a floury hand.

"Thanks a lot!" she said. "And I *don't* have to help him to the bathroom. He's perfectly capable on his own."

"I think it was beautiful, the reunion he had with Monsignor," Joan said.

"Yes!" Bernice said, "That's another reason I think he might be considering priesthood. He was really kind of enlightened by Monsignor. He said he'd been bitter and that a very ill patient had shown him how valuable it was to forgive. That very ill patient turned out to be our Monsignor."

"Really!" exclaimed Helen.

"Yes, and they were thrilled to see each other. I think Monsignor has really inspired him."

"What a beautiful story," said Joan.

"And how lucky that Monsignor is staying," said Annie. "I can see that being a blessing in so many ways."

"Father Bertrand was sure a blessing, too," Joan said. "Yesterday was quite a day at the military hospital."

"What did Father do?" Bernice said.

"Well, it's not a competition," said Annie, snickering. "I'm sure Monsignor's thing was just as good."

"Hit her for me, would you, Joan?" Bernice said. "And go on."

So Joan explained with great eloquence, very fitting of Christmas Eve, how Father's conversation with Bob had made him come around to the idea of re-entering society, even eager to do so, and especially with respect to sharing Laureen's company.

"Laureen said that Bob would have eventually relented, but maybe not getting the whole picture. Father's explanation helped him to be optimistic, rather than just accepting. That's what I love about it."

"I like that," Annie said. "I think I'll borrow that."

"Me, too," said Joan.

"Well, *I'm* certainly optimistic," said Helen, "and I sure would love to get more information about Harry, but I guess I've waited this long . . ."

"You know," said Bernice, "sometimes I feel like when you are optimistic, you kind of make good things happen."

"That's inspired," said Joan. "And I bet it's true!"

"Bob's folks are in Washington, aren't they?" Helen asked.

"Well, his mom passed away, and his father is a diplomat. I think he is posted somewhere in South America. I'm not sure. That's one of the reasons Laureen's parents made up a room for him."

"Oh, and I'm sure Laureen had nothing to do with it," Annie teased.

Joan laughed. "Probably a little! All of the joy that came with the lost and then regained love between those two has really given me that Christmas spirit. I know we have things to pray and hope for still, and of course we'd all love to see our men right here at home with us, but even as it is, it really seems like the Joy of Christmas has descended on us in some kind of delicate mist of happiness."

Annie wiped away a tear. "I don't think anyone could have said that better." She reached for Joan, who gave her a little hug. "We could use that happiness on Christmas Day for sure."

"Well I wonder if they might like to join us for Christmas Day," Helen said. "It would be so nice to see them together, especially after all of the turmoil!"

"Too late," said Joan. "I already asked them!"

"Nice," said Bernice. "Just go and invite whoever you want to someone else's house."

"Whom, whomever," said Annie. "Watch your language."

Everybody laughed.

"What was Laureen's answer?" Helen asked Joan.

"I think they'd love to come for a little while, and she said maybe she and Bob would drop something off beforehand."

"Oh they don't need to do that," said Helen. "As you girls can see, we'll be well-fixed for dessert, plus we have Annie's cheesecake coming."

"Wait!" Annie cried suddenly, tossing the hand towel onto the counter.

"No desserts?" Bernice asked. "Keepin' it all for yourself?"

"Listen," Annie continued, ignoring Bernice. "I had a dream last night and now I get what it was all about. What you said just reminded me—remember the missing chalice, Joanie? And ciborium?"

"Oh, from the Lithuanian church?" Joan answered.

"So cheesecake makes you think of chalices of Lithuania. . ." Bernice went on.

"Hit her for me, would you Helen?" Annie said. "Come on, Joanie, I think I just thought of where to look for the missing pieces! Get my wheelchair!"

That night, Midnight Mass was a glorious affair. Concelebrated by Father Bertrand and Monsignor Kuchesky in the light of 250 candles, and to the rich and wonderful sounds of the St. Benedict's Choir, Christmas Eve Mass uplifted the heart and mind of every attendee.

Joan looked for Laureen, and caught sight of her just before the choir started. They waved to each other, feeling the joy of so many things. Joan thought gently to herself how Faith had left her ready to welcome Christmas this year, no matter how things turned out. She prayed for life, for love, and the health in body and soul of all of the soldiers, but most especially for her very special soldier, wherever he may be.

Annie studied Joan as she knelt before Mass, deep in prayer, and looking so peaceful. This may all explode in our faces one day, and one day soon, she thought, but we'll be able to manage through it. Whatever the future brings, we have these moments, this joy, and our Faith, so strong and so sweet. She looked over at Bernice, who was making a face at her. "Right, Bernice?" she whispered.

"Right," said Bernice. She thinks I don't know what she was thinking, Bernice thought. But I bet it was good and peaceful thoughts. Every year, the glory of Jesus' birth has brought that joyful peace, and it will every year, no matter how things turn out. "Yeah," she said to Annie, "I hear you."

Helen, entrenched in her own thoughts, was startled by Bernice's sudden voice. "What?" she whispered.

"Oh nothing, just talking to Annie. Sorry," said Bernice.

Helen looked at the beautiful altar and the surrounding statues, flowers, and the glorious candlelight, piercing the darkness with each tiny but powerful flame. How precious this is, she thought, this time in this safe place in the world, how lucky we are to have such strong people fighting to protect this for us. She closed her eyes, picturing Harry, imagining him walking toward her, a vision of strength and comfort and precious love. Wherever it ends here, she thought, will not be the end of us. We will go on.

At the homily, Father Bertrand spoke on the gentle humanity that makes Christmas so possible each year, and on the hardness of life that makes it such a necessity each year. Then just when the congregation was moved to grateful tears, he asked Monsignor Kuchesky to speak briefly.

"Tonight," Monsignor said smiling, "when we, together Father and I, raise the chalice and the consecrated hosts tonight, we will be doing so in a very special way, out of gratitude to two fine young ladies in our parish. For many years, over 50 years, the royal family of Lithuania has been mourning the loss of ornaments specially made for them in Italy by very gifted Monks. They were lost during tumultuous years when they were moved out of the country for safekeeping. But through an amazing occurrence, and very happy coincidence, and with God's great blessings, two of our parishioners, Annie and Joan right here tonight, have discovered them in a secret compartment right here on the church grounds of St. Benedict's! Tonight, these ladies brought me the final pieces of the collection, our chalice and our ciborium, which we will use in celebrating our very beloved Christmas Eve Midnight Mass."

Joan, while embarrassed and beat red in the face, was delighted to be recognized.

She turned to Annie, who squeezed her hand and smiled, whispering, "Now *that's* a Christmas gift."

Bernice knocked her on the shoulder, "Go Annie and Joan!" she whispered. "Ain't no stoppin' you, even with a busted leg."

Helen elbowed Bernice. Bernice looked at Helen astounded, who laughed silently covering her mouth with her hand.

As the joyful parishioners exited the church, shaking hands and wishing each other happiest of holidays, Joan was startled to see Gloria Marini making her way purposefully toward them.

"Duck Joanie!" Bernice whispered.

"Shhh!" Helen said. "Hello, Gloria. Nice to see you, honey."

"Hello, Mrs. Ashenbach," Gloria said as warmly as she was able. "Merry Christmas."

"Why thank you. Merry Christmas to you, too!"

"I just wanted to come over to say hello and, the season and all, and didn't the choir sound nice tonight?" Gloria said, seeming to hunt for her words.

"Yes," said Bernice. "Very nice."

"I like the, those songs, the Christmas ones, you know," said Gloria.

"They're so nice," said Joan.

"Sort of appropriate for the season," Annie said under her breath.

Joan elbowed her. To Gloria, she said, "You look very nice tonight in your Christmas outfit!"

"Yes, she does!" said Helen.

"Thank you," said Gloria. "Well, okay, have a nice. . .time."

"You, too," said Helen. "Have a Merry Christmas."

The girls looked at each other, curious but unsure what to say.

"Remember," said Helen, as she turned Annie's wheelchair and they began to walk home.

"I know," said Bernice. "If it's not something nice, don't say nothing."

Joan giggled. "Yeah, something like that."

"I'm a little baffled is all I was going to say," said Annie.

"I think we're all a little baffled," said Bernice.

"Well I'm not," said Helen. "I think she was trying to make amends or maybe even make some friends."

"That's our first Christmas miracle," said Joan resolutely.

"Where did you find those last two pieces, anyway, miracle women?" Bernice asked.

"I was wondering the same thing," said Helen.

"Annie did it," said Joan. "She got a message from Heaven."

Annie smiled. "Maybe! I just got to thinking that following the fire, we've pretty much kept out of the back room because the floor's still a little wobbly. They've patched up that wall but not the floor. And I remember how it was that Joanie put her foot through it when we found the nativity scene. By the way, wasn't that beautiful?"

"It was darling!" said Helen. "I can see why it was so heartbreaking to them to lose it. A person could become quite attached to pieces that special."

"Yeah," Annie went on. "So anyway, we went back there this afternoon and Joanie tested other parts of that storage room and not surprisingly, there was another loose board not that far from the first one. And there was a second box inside! We were so excited. We didn't dare open it but took it straight over to the rectory. And I guess you know the rest."

By then, the congregation had dispersed into smaller groups, some walking down the streets to their homes, and others meeting up for midnight gatherings in friends' homes.

Helen and Bernice walked in front, and Joan took over the pushing of Annie's wheelchair. They lagged a little behind.

"This is like a little piece of Heaven," Joan said. "Don't you think?"

"I don't let myself imagine the beauty of Heaven. I can't do it," Annie said, startling Joan.

"You don't? Why not? It's such a happy thing to imagine."

"I think it's because so many things I've imagined through my life have turned out, well, they've been very nice, but never as great as I imagined them to be. I don't want to be disappointed in the ultimate thing."

"Heaven--God's House? Annie, that's the one thing you don't have to fear being disappointed in. There's no way you could possibly imagine how beautiful your home in Heaven will be. It's beyond our comprehension. You *can* imagine that one, Annie. Don't fear a thing, just imagine to your heart's content."

Annie breathed in the icy air and felt it fill her lungs in a new and exciting moment. "I love the sound of that. What a beautiful thought."

Chapter Twenty-Five

Christmas morning seemed to reach more deeply into hearts that year than ever before. While there was no snow, it seemed to be waiting for just the right time. The air was still and the sky was pristinely Christmas white. A lone paper boy delivered the Christmas Day edition, his bicycle so heavily laden that its squeaky axel delivered uneven yelps with each rotation. Only the occasional cardinal paid any attention to the mild thumps of newspapers landing on the various frozen surfaces.

At 6 North Edison, however, the women bustled joyfully, harmoniously preparing dishes for the great Christmas Dinner feast, such as it would be that year. The menu included a turkey, which was to be decorated with fresh vegetables when set out on the serving platter, in order to create the perception that it was a big bird, which it was decidedly not.

Also included would be the traditional mashed potatoes, and a fancy cheese, pasta, butter, and breadcrumbs dish, designed to look exotic when served in small red bowls that resembled Christmas bells. Most people knew it as macaroni and cheese.

Annie's family had sent two beautiful loaves of bread; one distinctly Italian, braided and sprinkled with sesame seeds, and a second which was rolled lengthwise, filled with cheddar, mozzarella and a third cheese the others had not heard of before, called ricotta.

Pickles of all sorts, made and stored the previous summer, harvested from their own Victory Garden would populate the buffet table at the back of the dining room. Annie wished that there would be olives, but not this year, she was told. Neither green nor black.

"It won't be this way forever," Helen had said that morning as she put an arm around Annie. "Before you know it, everyone will be back home, and we'll have everything we need."

Annie was so grateful for Helen. Without her, enduring this long absence and unknowing would have been agony. Helen never faltered. She was a strength that Annie hoped to one day be for her in return. When the news had come of Harry's imminent return, Annie had been ecstatic. Who better deserved such good news more than Helen, or Helen and Harry for that matter. He was a two-war veteran, carrying an incredibly heavy load about which the women knew very little, but Annie was sure his role was vital, even pivotal. And having served so well for so long, Harry deserved to be rewarded finally with time with his very beloved wife.

Nevertheless, Annie knew that the day that Harry came home, she would struggle not to yearn all the more for Sylvester. She could never forget the way her heart had sung at his unexpected appearance the previous year, and their blissful days together that had followed. To her, it had been one long day. What will it be like when he's home for good, she thought, and we never have to separate again? She could have teetered on the edge of fear that that might not come to be, but she no longer did, out of respect for Helen, and because of a Faith that had grown and strengthened through the year.

She moved her leg to try to keep it from going to sleep. "Four more weeks," she said to Joan, who had joined her at the table with a vegetable peeler. "Maybe I won't wait that long."

"You'd better if you don't want to be bowlegged," Joan said. "Listen to the doctor. That's why you went to him."

Helen laughed. "That's telling her, Joan."

"So how many are we?" Bernice asked. "Have we got a final count?"

"Well, there's the four of us," Helen said. "And Henry and his mom, that's six. Father and Monsignor, so eight. Then Bob and Laureen makes ten."

"That's a good number for Christmas dinner!" Joan said happily. "I love a nice big houseful on Christmas."

"Don't forget Margaret," said Annie. She smiled and gave Bernice a look. "She's bringing a date."

"What are you looking at me for?" Bernice said.

"You'd better keep your hands off this time," Joan teased.

"Oh girls, leave Bernice alone," Helen laughed.

"Maybe this will finally clear Margaret's misapprehension of how things were," Joan said. "Maybe she'll finally forgive you!"

Annie giggled.

"I don't know what you're laughing about," Bernice said to her. "You're the one who's going to find laundry detergent in your macaroni and cheese."

"So what did we stop at?" Helen asked. "Was it twelve?"

"Yes, with Margaret and her sergeant, it's twelve."

"I guess we'd better get this kitchen table in the dining room then," said Helen, "soon as we're done, and we'll set it up like an L."

"Oh that sounds nice," Joan said. "Everyone will be able to see everyone else."

As Helen and Bernice started to move things around, Annie grabbed Joan's arm. "Come here," she said. "I have something for you. I wasn't able to do anything for the others, but there's something I wanted you to have."

Joan turned her chair. "You do!" she said, eyes wide. "Is it my own personal cheesecake?"

"No, better!" Annie said. "Here."

Joan took the silver and purple bag from her. She recognized the Vespers Shop design and smiled. "I bet I know what it is!"

"Sorry I couldn't wrap it up all pretty," Annie said. "I didn't get to do much after the accident."

"Are you kidding?" Joan said, shaking her head and extracting the beautiful gift. It was St. Michael the Archangel, his sword drawn and pointing at the devil who flailed beneath him in defeat. The colors were striking, and his sword shimmered in a rich gold leaf.

Joan was aghast. "I've never seen it so close up before," she said, wiping away a tear. "It's magnificent Annie! Thank you."

She set it down and gave Annie a warm hug. "You are the best friend a girl could ever have!" she whispered.

"Hey, what are you guys up to over there?" Bernice called from the living room. "Who's giving out presents?"

"Me," said Annie. "Sorry I didn't get a chance to shop for everyone, but I knew something Joanie wanted and fortunately, it survived the fire."

"Well, unless I'm mistaken, you've given us cheesecake and some lush breads we would never have had without your generosity!" Helen said. "I think we're all pretty well covered from your corner."

"From everyone's corner," Joan said. "Let's put our beautiful St. Michael in the center of the table."

"Let me see him!" Bernice cried.

"What a beautiful statue of him," said Helen. "I want to get a better look when things quiet down."

Bernice took the statue in her hands and drew in her breath. She felt a sudden wave of emotion tied to an inspiration she had felt growing during her time caring for Henry. St. Michael, Heaven's fierce defender, was entrusted with the protection of souls from temptation and all evil. As Bernice studied the artist's representation of the saint, she felt a rededication to her calling, but this time with a purpose.

Helen stood next to her. "It's a beautiful statue, isn't it?" she said.

"While I was caring for Henry," Bernice said softly, "I had the feeling that I was kind of on the right track. I wasn't sure before just what I would do. I thought music, but how? I didn't see myself as a classroom teacher. But Henry started out so poorly and seeing him progress, improving to the point where he is now, I felt in alignment with that, I don't know, occupation, I guess."

"Are you saying you want to be a nurse?" Joan said, joining them.

"Yes, but I want to be a Sister, too. I want to help people heal, but be there for their hearts and souls, too. I guess like Monsignor Kuchesky was at first for Henry."

"Wow, Bern," said Annie. "That's something."

"Yeah," said Bernice, still studying St. Michael. "Since we've had to scale back the school idea, maybe we should add in a nursing section. After I learn how to do it myself, I can help other girls who want to follow this path."

"I think that's inspired," Helen said. "I really do. And at this time, I can't think of anything that is more needed."

Bernice smiled, finally looking up at her friends. "All right," she said. "I think I finally have my path!"

"How about hugs?" Helen said.

"I ain't asking," said Annie, moving into the huddle.

"Me, too!" said Joan.

Hours later, just as the turkey was ready to be placed on the platter, and one loaf of bread was about to go into the oven, the phone rang.

"I can't get it," said Annie who was setting the table with Bernice. "Joanie?"

"She's got her hands in the sink. I got it," Helen said.

She picked up the phone, turning down the music on the radio as she did so.

"Hello?"

"Sounds like a pahty awlready," came an unfamiliar voice.

"Uh. . ."

"I'm sorry, it's just I can hear the Christmas music. It sounds great!"

"Well. . . thank you," said Helen.

Joan turned toward Helen, her eyebrows raised.

"Ah I'm sorry! You don' know who I am! I'll make it shawt. I'm just cawlin' for a quick second wit Sly."

"Who?"

"Aw—sheee, oot," the man said. "I bet he ain't there yet. Shoot. Forget I said it, don't worry 'bout it."

"Well—"

"I'm so sorry! Bye! Merry Christmas!"

Joan dried her hands. The other girls remained involved in the business of setting up twelve chairs, arguing about how to best fit them around the L shape.

Joan tapped Helen on the shoulder. "Who was it?"

"I don't honestly know," said Helen, very honestly. But she knew what it meant. And she wasn't telling anyone. She looked at Joan with a twinkle in her eye. "I really don't know who that was."

"Who called?" Annie shouted from the dining room.

"Wrong number," Joan called back. But looking at Helen, she said softly, "Or so I assume."

Helen turned away, stifling a smile, but said nothing.

Just then Bernice ran to the window. "Look!" she said. "It's snowing!"

The four women gazed out Helen's large picture windows, watching the first few flakes flutter down and land invisibly on the ground.

"That's the real icy kind," Annie said. "It's the kind that sticks."

"Yep," said Joan nodding.

"Well, it's good our company doesn't have far to travel," Helen said. "And I'm glad in a way that Harry isn't coming today. I would be so worried that he'd make it all the way through the war and then have an accident in the snow."

"No car accident woulda stopped Harry," Annie said. "He's a tough guy."

Helen smiled, and Joan put an arm around her. "Let's hope everybody drives safely," she said, winking at Helen.

"Yeah," said Helen nodding enthusiastically.

"I just love to watch it snow," Bernice said. "It's so beautiful, so Christmas."

Before long, nearly everyone had arrived and were finding places around the table. Bernice and Annie had decided that there would have to be two heads to the L, since two ends of the table spots had been eliminated since they were pushed together. It left one seat looking at a wall mirror, and another facing the door.

"I'll sit at this spot," Helen said. "It's close to the kitchen, and since I need to see the door—"

"I'll sit there if you want," said Joan nudging her.

"No, that's all right, Joan," said Helen. "You sit beside me, here."

"I'll sit facing the wall," said Bernice, "I can make faces at myself in the mirror."

"If that amuses you," said Annie. "I'll sit beside you to make sure you don't get carried away."

Henry laughed, "See," he said to his mother, "I told you these girls look out for each other."

Henry sat on Bernice's other side, and his mother next to him.

Monsignor and Father were enjoying the banter, and chuckled as they found places around the table.

"I guess we can get started," Helen said, taking the turkey from Joan and putting it on the table.

"What about Margaret and her date?" Annie asked.

"She's coming a little later," Helen said. "Maybe we should make them a couple of plates."

"Sure," Bernice said. "I'll do it."

"Sit down, Joan, I think we're all ready."

After Joan and Helen were seated, Father Bertrand said a special grace giving thanks for the blessings of the dear and beloved company, but also asking blessings on those less fortunate, who struggled for food or warmth, or even survival. Monsignor Kuchesky then thanked God again for the lovely feast and for the miraculous find of the blessed chalice and ciborium, which he would return to Lithuania when it was considered safe to do so.

After Grace, Father said, "That was truly a miracle for them to be found just in time to be used for their original purpose, to glorify the Lord at Christmas."

"It was a miracle," nodded Monsignor.

Just then, as Helen picked up the knife to cut into the turkey, the front door shot open and there, like a picture out of the past stood a snow-covered Harry. Restraining himself from bursting into the room, he called out, "Is this Helen's home for wayward soldiers?"

Instantly Helen was on her feet, heading for the door.

"Helen, put down the knife!" called Annie.

"Oh," she said, slowing down long enough to drop it onto the table beside Annie.

Harry chuckled, an unceasing glow in his eyes and arms wide, striding toward his wife. They embraced, instantly in a world of their own, shutting out all struggles, all the long hours of worry and pain. Only the two of them existed in that moment, along with light, happiness, and peace.

After what seemed like a pretty long time to the guests and about four or five seconds to Harry and Helen, Henry cleared his throat. "Uh Sir, I think the turkey's getting cold."

The room was filled with laughter.

"Who said that?" Harry asked in his harshest fake voice.

"I did, Sir, Sergeant Henry Harper, R Company, Fifth Army."

"Well, nice to meet you," said Harry, extending his hand across the table.

Everyone laughed again.

"Let's shut the door and keep the cold air out," Helen said. "Harry take off your coat and sit down over here."

Joan got up. "Here, Harry, sit here," she said, smiling so hard she was nearly crying.

Annie looked down, a smile on her face, but tears in her eyes. *Don't cry, don't cry* she told herself.

Harry said "I'm coming in, but I gotta get my stuff. Hold on."

Helen looked at Joan. *Again?* their expressions seemed to say. But Helen was not waiting for any grand entrance if there should be one. Instead, she headed for the door. "I'll give you a hand," she said to Harry.

"Oh that's okay, Honey," said Harry. "I can manage."

"Well, let me hold open the door, then," she said.

He looked up at her in time to see her knowing smile.

"Well all right," he said chuckling at her.

Motioning around the corner, he signaled to someone who eagerly joined them at the door.

"Sly!" said Annie. "Sly!" she said again. She tried to stand up and fell back onto her seat, and then tried again, with the same result.

"Your leg's broke," Bernice whispered in her ear.

"Oh yeah," said Annie.

Sly's expression, which had been one of overwhelming joy turned suddenly to fear and concern as he flew into the room, forgetting that he also had a bad leg. The result was less tragic than it was comical, as he plopped awkwardly into the fortunately empty chair on the near side of Annie. Unfortunately, he did so with such enthusiasm that both it and Annie's chair, captured in the inertia, toppled over backward, and landed, both humans intact, yet no worse for the wear.

The other guests would observe an assortment of casts, bandages, and tangled arms and legs, but two faces laughing, kissing, and crying hysterically that would be described on succeeding Christmases for many years to come.

"Are you guys alright?" asked Bernice standing over them.

"Of course they're all right," said Joan, laughing and crying right along with them. "But how long are you going to stay down there?"

Annie and Sly began to laugh all over again. "Not sure," Annie managed to say.

"Cap, could you give us a hand?" Sly asked. "Not that it ain't great fun and all." He gave Annie another kiss. "That's one thing I'm never going to stop doing," he whispered in her ear.

"You're right about that," Annie whispered back.

"Is that a married couple?" Monsignor asked Father.

Everyone laughed.

"We're not legal yet," Sly called from the floor, "but it won't be long now!"

When Annie and Sly had been gently disentangled and sat more comfortably beside each other at the table, Helen asked everyone to take their seats again, and giving Sly a kiss, asked Annie for the knife, which had maintained its place on the table throughout their adventure.

"Honey," she said smiling at Harry, "How would you like to slice the turkey?"

"I would love it," he said. "We don't want to keep Sgt. Harper waiting."

"I'd appreciate that, Sir," said Henry.

The table was alive with laughter and the rich heart-stopping joy of answered prayers when, before

Harry had time to make that first cut, another knock came at the door.

Joan's heart leaped. It can't be, she thought. It's too much to hope for.

"Well," said Monsignor quietly, "I think we're going to have to heat up that gravy."

Father Bertrand chuckled.

"Who else is coming?" Sly asked Annie.

"Bob and Laureen were supposed to come," she answered, but there was a kind of hesitation in her voice. She turned to Joan, looking wistfully.

Oh, thought Joan. That's who it is, of course. Her heart slowed down a few paces.

Helen was on her feet again for the seemingly never-ending hostess duty of answering the door. "Oh hello Bob, Laureen, and oh!" she said with a cry.

Everyone was startled, and looked to see if she'd maybe tripped on the threshold. But quickly the answer was visible, as a third party approached the door, carefully stepping up from the outside stoop and into the doorway. Helen reached out instinctively, unable to resist grasping the thin but remarkably steady hand of the handsome soldier.

No one said a word. Everyone, including the soldier, looked at Joan. But in the silence, Joan had shut her eyes. It couldn't be true. And if it was not true, she couldn't bear it.

She stood up, hands at her sides, slowly opening her eyes into the silence. And there he was. A man, strong and handsome, but very much thinner than she had remembered. Still he was as handsome as it took to completely take away her breath. Just as she thought she might faint, Joan heard him say, "Joan, uh. . . what's for dinner?"

In the laughter that followed, Joan trembled her way toward her handsome Sergeant Dick Thimble. He was thin, and his beautiful dark eyes seemed to be even richer in wisdom, yet still dancing with the humor from which he was seemingly inseparable.

In their embrace, Joan saw him alone, wounded, rescued, and returned to her as if watching a movie made just for her. "I was so scared I'd never see you again," she whispered to him.

"I'd never let that happen," he whispered back. Then pausing said, "No matter what you fixed for dinner."

She bubbled up with laughter as they struggled to find a place together at the table.

"Take my chair, Honey," Helen said. "Harry, get another one from the kitchen, would you, honey?"

"I guess I can breathe again now," Joan said softly to Dick. "Now that I see you, alive."

"Me, too," he said. "I never stopped thinking of you, not even for a second. There's so much to tell, but for now, let's just be here."

"Yes, and we'll stay close."

"Very close."

"Indivisible."

"Absolutely."

"Oh, Laureen," said Joan. "Bob! I'm so sorry. I didn't mean to ignore you."

Everyone laughed, and as Helen finally cut the turkey and Bernice reheated the gravy, a bountiful Christmas dinner was finally begun.

An hour later, as the dinner wound down, Sly called out, "Hey Cap, you still got any of those cigars?"

Dick's ears perked up. "Cigars?"

"You've got a lot of cigar fans in this crowd, Captain Ashenbach," said Bob.

"Hey, that's Harry. I'm just about out now, gonna have to get used to be plain old Harry. Might as well start right now."

"Henry's not having any," Bernice said. "He's not supposed to smoke until he's 100%."

"Aw, Bernice," said Henry. "Who said that?"

"You know who, the doctor."

"Practicing, Bern?" Annie asked.

"Practicing?" said Henry. "What's that?"

"Maybe Bernice liked her experience with nursing," Henry's mother said. "She was certainly good at it!"

Bernice smiled shyly. "I think," she said looking at Monsignor, "I will get some advice, but I am inspired right now to be a nursing Sister."

Monsignor smiled, raised his eyes to heaven and whispered a silent thanks.

"You'll be the best there is," Henry said, taking her hand. "I'm walking proof."

"Yes, *walking* proof," said his mother.

As the girls cleared away the things, except for Annie, who had yet to release Sly from her side, Dick and Bob lit their cigars and took seats in the living room.

"You're looking even better today, buddy," said Bob.

"You, too. I didn't think you were going to keep that leg. I hardly noticed any limp when you got out of the car."

"Yeah, it's there. I gotta take it easy for a while, but apparently I will be good as new eventually."

"I can't thank you enough, buddy, for letting them know they needed to get me to Evac," Dick said. "I'd a been a goner."

"And I woulda been if you hadn't hit that sniper. Remember that dream you told me about yesterday, when you were laid up in Oklahoma?"

"Yeah, thank God it was only a dream."

"You know, Dick, it wasn't only a dream. You know how I was fading away when you were trying to reach me? That was happening right here. I couldn't get a grip. I was all wrung out with guilt and shame of leaving you behind."

Dick lowered his head. "We're going to have these thoughts," he said. "I was imagining what it would be like for all of us who survive. I think the dream was about that, too. But let's not spoil it for the girls. We don't need them to go through anymore. I thought," he sighed. "I thought my Joan was going to faint away this evening when I showed up."

Bob chuckled. "She might just have!"

In the kitchen, Joan hugged Laureen. "I can't believe it's happening," she said. "I feel like my feet aren't quite touching the ground."

"Let me see," said Laureen looking down at Joan's feet. "Oh look at that! They're not!"

They giggled. "I'm sure you're wondering how this all came about," Laureen said. "Bob knew he was here yesterday, but he kept it to himself. He saw the medical plane and he knew one of the patients because he saw Dick's Indian blanket."

"His Indian blanket?" Joan asked.

"I think he's had it all his life. Anyway, he needed some time with him. Those guys have gone through a lot, Joan," she said.

"I know it," Joan said. "I can feel it and I can see it, but it's like you said. We're the same, but we're different, and I agree that we're just going to have to let them either share it or not as they see fit."

"Yep," said Laureen, putting an arm around her. "They have each other. But we also have each other."

Joan smiled. She looked at Annie and Bernice, both happily engaged in conversations of their own. "We are so lucky. We will always have one another," she said.

"That we will," said Helen with a smile, entering the kitchen. "This is so much happiness, we're going to have to figure out a way to package and preserve it!"

They carried out the desserts and dessert dishes and set them around the table. Just as Helen was about to sit down again, a knock came at the door.

Everyone looked around. "But. . ." said Joan innocently, "we're all here!"

Everyone laughed.

"Maybe it's Santa," said Father Bertrand.

Amidst the ensuing gaiety, Helen opened the door to Margaret and her new date, whom she introduced as Sergeant Elwood Blank.

"Well, nice to meet you," said Helen. "Come on in, you're just in time for dessert."

"We were given the timetable," Margaret said. "So we are fortunate that it coincided with your schedule."

"Yes, we estimated based on the average amount of time one engages in completing a meal," Sgt. Blank said, "and then multiplied by two factors, including the

holiday element, and the added number of attendees."
He smiled at Margaret. "Looks like our equation was
spot on," he said.

"Perfectly appropriate," said Margaret.

Overhearing the entire conversation, Bernice gave
Annie the okay sign and giggled.

"Didn't I tell you?" Annie whispered. "But just
keep your hands off this time."

"What'd she say?" asked Henry.

"Nothing," said Bernice, winking at him. "She just
wants to make sure that we all followed the right
path."

As the party sat down for dessert, and the curtains
were closed to disguise their light from enemy eyes,
the joy on that Christmas day, despite the snow and the
cold, and the War that carried on, brought forth a new
birth of Faith, Hope, and Love in Abbotsville.

The End.

Indivisible Hearts
is <u>Book 3</u> in the Serve Series by Cece Whittaker.

Find <u>Books 1 and 2</u> (and soon, Book 4!) at:
www.CeceWhittakerStories.com

I truly appreciate your reading my stories and keeping these characters alive in our hearts! Thank you!

Cece Whittaker, 2019.

Made in the USA
Coppell, TX
14 January 2020